RHIANNON HEINS

STORY of SOUL

Tales of waking up in the dreamscape
and unlocking the magic of incarnation

Story of Soul – Tales of Waking Up in the Dreamscape and Unlocking the Magic of Incarnation
© 2025 Rhiannon Heins

All rights reserved. No part of this publication may be reproduced, stored in a retrieval system, or transmitted in any form or by any means—electronic, mechanical, photocopying, recording, or otherwise—without the prior written permission of the copyright holder, except in the case of brief quotations embodied in critical articles and reviews.

First Edition

Published in Australia by Barefoot and Thriving, operating the business of Intuitive Rebirth under license from Rhiannon and Scott Heins as trustees for Intuitive Rebirth Trust.

ISBN: 978-0-646-73247-3

Cover and interior design © Barefoot and Thriving

This book is a work of spiritual nonfiction and memoir that blends lived experience with visionary storytelling. While inspired by real events and people, certain details have been adapted or fictionalized for privacy, narrative flow, and symbolic meaning. The views expressed reflect the author's personal beliefs and experiences of spiritual and metaphysical phenomena and are offered for inspiration and reflection only—not as professional advice or a substitute for medical, psychological, or other professional care. Readers are encouraged to approach the material with discernment and to seek their own understanding and guidance where appropriate.

Chapter One

As the bass of the speakers thundered through the earth and up my legs, my heart cracked open. It cracked open to my fellow partygoers who, in that single moment in time, shared a common thread of understanding—this was it, this was what we existed for, a moment separate from the monotony, where life was perfect. The sun set through the ancient trees guarding the amphitheatre, and the searing heat of the Australian December day eased with the gentle blow of a dusk breeze. I was home. I stood at the top level of the amphitheatre and looked down over the pulsing hum of the collective, dancing as one beat, one rhythm, one human family. The DJ was the conductor, not just of the music but of the people, united in one dance, unified by a thousand smiles of ecstasy.

And then it happened. The hypnotic deep bass disappeared into nothingness, and a silence fell through the amphitheatre, making space for the dusk bird calls to echo across the valley. A familiar harmony sounded through the speakers—the saxophone of George Michael's "Careless Whisper"—to cut through the intensity of a whole day of drum and bass. A moment to pause and feel the simplicity of a song my parents once listened to on their CD player in the living room. Why did this moment feel so incredible? Love, nostalgia and the sweet memories of my family flooded through my body. Who knew I loved "Careless Whisper" so deeply? The saxophone moved through my cells, merging me with the trees that surrounded me, uniting me with the sky and the clouds that felt so close to me. My heart was opened even further. I pondered, surely I couldn't be any more in love with life than right now? But with a purposeful pull of a menthol cigarette and a sudden rush of nicotine colliding with the MDMA peaking in my body, it got just that little better. Just when I thought that my heart was so full of love that it'd explode, the bass dropped, and the collective dance of the enlivened souls at the festival dropped with it. That moment will forever be remembered in the fabric of my cells. I was home. This was what I lived for. The love. The unity. The pulse. The beat.

As time went on, I longed for more of the aliveness that I felt on that beautiful festival day. I chased that moment repeatedly. But the moment never came. Perhaps another pill? Or another party? Maybe another festival? But the more I chased the love, oneness and connection that I experienced on that day, the further I fell from it. And fall, I did.

My drug of choice was MDMA. It felt like it pulled at the fabric of my body, softening and dissolving the layers that kept me separate from experiencing true connection. True connection was what I craved. I wanted to feel the people surrounding me in a shared, wholehearted intimacy of innocence. I longed to see into their hearts to uncover both their pain and their love. I sought to know them beyond the invisible guarding that both they and I had created, so that together we could share in a moment of pure truth. My ache for connection was agonising. I wanted to merge with every moment, dissolving the past and future, and suspend myself in a heaven where nothing else existed. And the more I used MDMA as a vessel of connection, the more separate I felt in my normal daily reality. The higher I got on the weekend, the more painful the low during my working week.

It was a weekly spiritual comedown that shattered me a little more each time. A slow-burning dark night of the soul where the dullness of my existence pulled me into a shadowy trench of my deepest pain.

I quickly realised that the weekly ritual of drug-induced escapism wasn't doing anything to remedy the inner pain that was unravelling from within the depths of my body and psyche. I had a hint of wisdom that spoke through my compartmentalised life, telling me to aim higher, try harder and do better.

I met an inner wisdom that grieved my most self-destructive actions. I met within myself a heart of purity that ached with disappointment every time I hurt my body through poor choices. Sorry waves of sadness would flood through me, wrapping me in the loving embrace of my inner mother of self, urging me to remember my divinity. Alongside the purity of my sadness birthed from my eternal love for self, I held within me immense shame that plagued my mind with judgement and self-loathing. The shame made it hard to look my parents in the eyes over dinner. The visceral shame that I carried within me held a nauseating quality that overshadowed all other embodied sensations. But I also had a knowing that the shame I was experiencing was a gift, an emotional weight of suffering at a magnitude that would drown me in the pits of sorrow if I didn't set it free. I knew the shame was a gift holding the fire of potential for my liberation.

And so, with shame as my sacred catalyst for alchemy, I found a path to true liberation.

This story is a journey of liberation. My liberation, your liberation, humanity's liberation.

This is the story of how I came to feel the drumbeat of the earth pulse through my body in the silent prayer of a single moment. This is the story of how I came to feel the pain, the pleasure and the joy of my fellow brothers and sisters of this sacred humanity through no other gateway than our own pure intention. This is the story of how I cracked my heart open so wide that I died, only to be reborn—completely alive.

Our ancestors of all lineages sat around the fire and told stories. Stories of remembering and healing, stories of connection. Stories of death and of rebirth. Stories of this world and stories of the dreamscape. What is a story if not a journey? A journey that has the power to move you from lost to alive, from fighting to surrendering, from wanting to being.

It is with deep honour that I invite you on this journey. A ceremony of releasing, remembering and rising.

Let's begin.

Chapter Two

If a story is just a journey told, then there is no better place to begin than at the beginning—in the mythic realm that to the mind appears like a dream but to the spirit feels like the eternal truth.

I am here on this Earth, in this reality, to heal and awaken, but what is it I am awakening to? I am here to know myself, but what is the "self" that I am here to know?

Now, I will begin the story.

It all began with nothing. No thing, no one, no where. Just the infinite Eternal Ocean of Light pulsing with the potential of all possibilities. The Eternal Ocean of Light was pure peace and love, with no future nor past, and yet it had a consciousness, a knowing that could decide and could birth all things into being. The Eternal Ocean of Light pondered to itself, "What if I were to forget, for just a moment, the infinite peace and love that I am? How much more deeply would I feel the bliss of my beingness in my inevitable remembering? What would this journey of forgetting and remembering be, since I am all that is, was and will ever be?"

Anything the Eternal Ocean of Light pondered over would manifest into form in an instant, since its essence was that of pure creative potential. This creative potential was a pulsing ember of limitless possibility, awaiting the spark of conscious thought to fully ignite it. Suddenly, the Eternal Ocean of Light flashed as its frequency of potential burst into a surge of creation. From nothingness, a dreamscape was birthed. A dreamscape for the sole and absolute purpose of the Eternal Ocean of Light, forgetting and remembering its own simple nature.

The Eternal Ocean of Light sparked into form individualised spirits, all of them seeded with the mission of forgetting and remembering their true nature. The Eternal Ocean of Light named these individualised spirits "souls" and set the souls free into the dreamscape to have experiences beyond simply being the peace and love that they were.

The souls needed a realm within the dreamscape to have experiences, and so a realm of physicality with trees, rocks, a sky, air, water, fire and soil was instantly exploded into form. The souls needed physical bodies to have experiences in this physical realm, so physical bodies were created for them to inhabit while they experienced forgetting and remembering the Eternal Ocean of Light that was their true nature.

The realm of physicality within the dreamscape was named Earth, and the physical vessels through which the souls experienced physicality were called human bodies. The souls combined with the body vessels were simply named human beings. Human beings took two distinct forms, man and woman. Each of the two distinct forms had its own essence of unique gifts, strengths and attributes that would assist in the journey of forgetting and remembering.

From the frequency of nothingness and pure potential, a fully manifest dreamscape realm was birthed, sparked into form for the singular purpose of souls forgetting and then remembering their truth, as an aspect of the eternal one.

Earth, the realm of physicality, had a concept of linear time to assist with the mission of forgetting and remembering. On Earth, time could be measured in days, by the sun; months, by the moon; or years, by the rotation of the stars. The sun, the moon and the stars had secret messages written within them to assist the human souls to remember once they had fallen into the depths of their forgetting.

The human body was not eternal. So the souls would choose to visit the realm of physicality for a set duration of time that was a single incarnation within one human body. Within this set period of time, the soul would have a mission depending on its stage within the journey of forgetting and remembering. This soul mission would involve learning what is truly real and where all perceived life truly arises from—the Eternal Ocean of Light where all is peace and love.

As each individualised soul experienced more and more unique incarnations, some souls fell into the pits of forgetting, for life in the realm of physicality was full of pleasures and powers that are unique to the dreamscape. Some souls incarnated many times with a complete disregard for the original assignment of the mission and instead became hungry to fulfil the insatiable desires of the human body vessel and its own will. This will of the human, void of the soul mission and its original assignment, was called "ego".

But of course the Eternal Ocean of Light already knew itself, and so the assignment required a forgetting before a remembering, so the birth of "ego" was always needed. Otherwise, there was no need for the birthing of the realm of experience and physicality in the first place. But once the human being was completely identified with the ego, and had lost all connection and association to the original mission, they were at the stage of the assignment where they had utterly forgotten. And thus the journey of remembering would begin.

When the human being had completely forgotten the soul essence of itself and the origin of self as the Eternal Ocean of Light, the man or woman would experience immense suffering. The suffering was a necessary process to trigger the journey of remembering. The absolute identification with the realm of physicality was embedded with a frequency of suffering because it was void of the peace and love of the Eternal Ocean of Light. If a man or woman purposefully denied the Eternal Ocean of Light, the guidance system that helped each soul in its sacred mission was inaccessible, and the realm of physicality turned into a prison of suffering for the mind and body.

From the prison of self-perpetuated suffering, the man or woman fuelled by ego became lost, helpless and full of fear. The fear would stop the man or woman from receiving guidance from the Eternal Ocean of Light, and complete isolation would set in.

The Eternal Ocean of Light ceaselessly monitored the journey of each soul, no matter how deeply they fell into the pits of forgetting. The Eternal Ocean of Light was always weaving a current or a frequency of the path that should be taken to fulfil the soul mission. This frequency was easy to feel and attune to when the soul was on its path of remembering. But when the soul had deeply forgotten, the Eternal Ocean of Light would have to send a powerful experience of destruction or chaos to ensure the soul oriented back onto the correct path.

When the realm of physicality known as Earth would enter phases and cycles of mass forgetting, where great numbers of souls were led by ego alone, the Eternal Ocean of Light would ensure necessary experiences within the dreamscape were triggered to catalyse some kind of mass remembering of the true nature of the spirit. Accidents, natural disasters, sickness, tragedy—all manner of experiences within the Earth realm would be activated to help catalyse the lost souls back onto the path of their missions. The purpose of these major events was to move the ego-led being into a place of desperation, whereby the helpless got onto their knees and asked for help. Help of whom? Help of the one who was always listening, the Eternal Ocean of Light.

Once help had been requested, it was always granted. And a stream of events, encounters and experiences would be synchronistically orchestrated for the human being to remember the soul nature and to trust once again in the divine power of the Eternal Ocean of Light.

These moments were called the "dark night of the soul". These were the instances when a human being would fall into the pits of suffering within the realm of physicality, where they had no choice but to ask for help from a power beyond their own will. This prayer for help was deemed the first sacred step of remembering, and it would catalyse the rest of the pathway home, back to the Eternal Ocean of Light.

Lifetime after lifetime, the soul would go back to the realm of physicality to learn more, balance karmic debts and remember the eternal, true, loving nature of self. Once the mission was absolutely fulfilled by one soul and the soul completely identified with the Eternal Ocean of Light that it truly was, it would no longer be individualised as a soul and would once again be infinite peace, with no beginning nor end.

Once all souls had fulfilled their mission, there would be no dreamscape realm of physicality since it would not be needed. That was unless the Eternal Ocean of Light decided otherwise.

Chapter Three

Now, before I keep going with the tale of the dreamscape and the souls within it, I'll share with you a tale of my own.

The taxi door opened, and out of it stepped the man to whom I had devoted my life for the previous three years. Just a week prior, his presence held within it a familiar contentment that felt like certainty and stability. But with a single step of his rubber flip-flop onto the scorching bitumen ground outside the hotel lobby, his arrival stirred within me something new—a sickening discomfort I'd never before known. This relationship was done. I knew it, but the warmth of his heartfelt embrace after a week of separation made it glaringly obvious he had no idea what was coming.

A month earlier, he and I had visited the Fremantle Markets. It was an eclectic market with a blend of artisan food, local art and dusty CD stalls. He had no interest in the arts, and all that was sacred and lovable about the market appeared to be lost on him. He did, however, delight at the sight of the giant pancake cafe. While he ordered his Nutella and banana filled crepe, I wandered over to the tarot stall. Ever the mystic, the glimpse of the draping red velvet fabric hanging loosely from a curtain pole lured me in. The chalkboard sign read, "10-minute readings for $10." How could I refuse? The tarot reader was young and beautiful. She looked far too normal for me to trust the value of her mysticism. But still, ten dollars for ten minutes, whatever she had to say, it was going to be more interesting than waiting in line for a giant pancake.

I took my seat at the low stall, stooped over the wooden table, waiting for my fortune to be revealed. "Do you have a question?" she enquired, staring deeply into my eyes as she shuffled the cards.

I shrugged. I did not have a question, but I replied, "I suppose I'd like to know what my future holds."

She stopped shuffling the cards and split the deck into three piles on the table, where she continued to turn over a series of ten cards systematically. The cards themselves meant nothing to me, but they spoke to her very clearly.

"He's coming," she said with unwavering certainty and excitement. She appeared delusionally thrilled for me. "The man is coming." She continued, "A great love is coming. And he will be here very soon."

I laughed. This woman was clearly useless and a fraud, I thought to myself. No wonder this was only ten dollars. I let her know that I already had a boyfriend, thanked her politely and left to go and find him.

"How was it?" he enquired, mid-mouthful of pancake.

"Shit," I responded definitively.

Shit was a common word I would have used to describe many experiences, places and things at the time. The euphoric highs experienced in the depth of the night tend to leave a stain of discontentment on even the sweetest and most well-meaning aspects of the day. I had found myself living a strange, otherworldly blend of spiritual mysticism and substance-induced escapism. A dance floor of lost inhibitions in one moment and a yoga mat of tears and prayers of forgiveness in the next. I was trying to find balance. I was trying so hard to find my way. But what I didn't realise was that my way was finding me.

My mum invited me on a spontaneous mother-daughter trip to Bali. The first of its kind. A week of juice cleansing, yoga, meditation and healing. I said yes without a thought, knowing that once we'd completed a week of fasting, my boyfriend and my dad would come and join us, and together as a foursome we could have a relaxing holiday, likely undoing all the good work done on the cleanse.

Before I knew it, my mum and I were arriving in the mecca of modern spirituality—Ubud. A place where the potent energy of the land, the prayer and the culture silently weave their way through the smog-filled streets. Where the smoke of the incense and the chiming prayer bells collide with the honking of a hundred scooter horns. It was intense, but I loved it. It felt as though Ubud had called me for healing, and I was right where I needed to be.

My mum and I wasted no time—we did everything. Gong healings, kundalini yoga, breathwork, power yoga, Balinese massage. We did not stop. Green juices, wheatgrass shots and young coconuts. I felt so alive. Lying flat upon my back on yoga studio floors, I sobbed more that week than ever before in my life. Day by day, I was opening and softening.

On one particular afternoon after a devotional singing class, something happened that would change my life forever. I found my mum sitting on a stool outside the juice bar talking to a man. As I approached them, the man looked familiar, although I'd never seen him before in my life. I sat down with them, and the stranger introduced himself as Scott.

He was beautiful. His eyes sparkled blue-green, and his gaze softly landed in the depths of my consciousness—the space where it seemed I'd known him for an eternity. Our conversation instantly flowed, and I felt as though I never wanted it to end. We spoke of our love of yoga, Gregg Braden's *Missing Links* show on the Gaia network and Wim Hof breathwork. I'd never met a man like him. He was soft, gentle and unpretentious. He was a man's man with the arms and hands of a worker and the heart of a philosopher.

Hours passed by as Scott and I sat suspended in conversation, with my mum watching on in quiet observation of the palpable chemistry.

For the remainder of the week, I spent as much time with Scott as possible. I told him about my boyfriend back home, and with a moral boundary preventing us from exploring our strongest energetic desires, we allowed a friendship to blossom. This friendship took us on a week-long journey of profound conversations where we shared our deepest fears and dreams with one another. A friendship of shared power yoga and sound healings. A friendship that felt ancient, like we were picking up where we'd left off.

Each night, Scott enchanted my dream space. I'd dream of our future children and golden threads interconnected between our heart spaces. I had never before believed in "the one", but if there were such a thing, Scott was it.

On the final night before my mum and I left Ubud, I said goodbye to Scott. We had to leave to meet my boyfriend and my dad; the holiday would continue on as though this encounter had never happened. As I parted ways with Scott, a lump grew in my throat and didn't leave for the remainder of the day.

It was time to journey to the restaurant strip of Canggu, where the medicine frequency of Ubud was just a distant dream. Into a matrix of holiday makers, my mum and I arrived, followed shortly after by the taxi carrying my boyfriend. He'd arrived. Not to the woman he'd left, but to someone new. I had fundamentally changed for good. For the better. I was done with the life I had been living. The life my boyfriend represented was finished.

I had been opened through purity of heart and true depth of connection. I didn't need to escape anymore because I'd felt something organic within me that was home. I'd felt my own love and my own truth and felt the power of it being mirrored back to me in another. I'd felt freedom, and I wasn't going to slip back into the cave of isolation that was my life with my boyfriend.

And so the moment we checked into our room, I told him everything and sent him home. He told me that he had asked my dad for permission to propose and had a ring in his backpack, but truly, I did not care. I wanted him gone. Out of my life now. I had found a way to choose me. And I knew that this man did not choose the true me. He chose a lifestyle that I worked well with so long as I remained shut off from my divinity and power.

A surge of divine courage moved through me. I was unmovable on a new, higher path that had unfolded before me. I felt as though I was being guided so powerfully that the breakup was orchestrated for me. Every word I uttered, every step I took—it was all taken care of, and I just needed to surrender and let go of the reins.

Suddenly I found myself in Bali, alone and unattached. And I sent a simple email that would change everything—"Scott, I'm single. Where are you? I'll come and meet you."

And meet we did, this time without the moral limitations of another relationship. We were free to take the lid off our overflowing bottled chemistry and explore where this chemistry would take us.

Five weeks later, I was pregnant.

Chapter Four

The previous story is the true tale of how my beloved husband and I met. A true love story of synchronicity and divine orchestration, typical of any romance novel. But indeed, aren't we all just living a curated existence wherein each person is the main character of their own story? I certainly didn't write or curate the story that brought me to the point in time where I was pregnant and madly in love with a man I'd only met five weeks prior, and yet I participated fully in creating that experience.

So who is the curator of the stories we live? Stories so wondrous we couldn't dare think them up. Stories so exhilarating that they are copied by fiction authors. Who is the great author, the great curator of tales and weaver of synchronicities? Well, I have a tale to share with you about just that. It is a tale that continues on from the previous story of the Eternal Ocean of Light.

As you know, the Eternal Ocean of Light was simply peace and presence, with no beginning and no end. When the Eternal Ocean of Light birthed a dreamscape and souls to experience the dreamscape, for the purpose of temporarily forgetting and then remembering the pure peace and presence that it was, this inception moment was named the moment of Creation.

The energy that easily and effortlessly birthed the dreamscape and the souls into being from eternal nothingness was named Creation Energy. The Eternal Ocean of Light witnessed such beauty within Creation Energy, it was as though Creation Energy in and of itself was something to admire. Mirrored back to the Eternal Ocean of Light from its emanating admiration was a female figure, a goddess of gargantuan stature. Creation Energy was a feminine spirit, and she was spectacular. She was neither young nor old; she was ageless. She was neither soft nor fierce—she was Creation and she was perfect. Her essence was fluid, and she moved in a rhythm of harmony with all she had created. Her hair flowed in great cosmic lengths, which danced, wrapped and waved around all she had created. In her essence, she was love, and thus she loved everything she brought into existence. She was the Great Mother of all things, and she watched in wonder of her creation—the dreamscape and all within it, her beloved children.

The Great Mother of creation loved every human being within the dreamscape to the absolute fullest of a mother's capacity. Her love had no limits, and it was powerful, for the Great Mother's love also held within it the infinite blessing of the Eternal Ocean of Light.

The Eternal Ocean of Light seeded each soul with a mission within the dreamscape, but the Great Mother ensured that each of her children received as much support and guidance as possible to make the fulfilment of that mission not only an achievable task, but a beautiful one.

The Eternal Ocean of Light presented the mission, clear and simple, and the Great Mother orchestrated and arranged everything she could within the dreamscape to align all necessary factors for each human soul to thrive and succeed with the mission. Her ability to create was limitless. Her genius in her creation was unfathomable. She wove a tapestry of perfectly aligned events, synchronicities and encounters within the dreamscape, and with the pull of a single thread, all of her children would experience a miracle simultaneously.

The Great Mother would pause clocks and watches so the fabric of linear time would reset simply so that one of her children could be exactly where they needed to be in a precise moment to receive a surprise gift that would change the course of their life forever.

The Great Mother would slam closed doorways of opportunity, regardless of how crushing the perceived loss would be to her child. The Great Mother would stop at nothing to prevent her child from following the wrong path—so ferocious was her love.

The Great Mother could see clearly the faults within each of her children, and she loved them all, regardless. However, where there was delusion, pain or fear, the Great Mother would guide her children in the direction that ensured each of these faults was faced and transformed. The Great Mother knew that her love would sometimes lead her children down a treacherous path, but that path, which was always the path to freedom, had to be walked.

The Great Mother knew her children so well. She knew that each of them related to her differently. Some of her children felt her presence in the purest aspects of the dreamscape—the natural environments where the elements moved freely, such as the oceans, the rivers, the mountains and the meadows. And so she would guide these children day by day, deeper into nature. Some of her children felt her presence most when they closed their eyes and spent time in the solitude of their own hearts. And so for these children, she would guide them to meditate, to pray and to cherish their solitude. Some of her children felt her presence most in their connection with others, in dance, play and fun. And so she would guide these children into community and into the warm embrace of souls who vibrated at the same pulse.

The Great Mother spoke to all her children, in whatever way she knew they listened. She would ensure a song would come through the radio at the perfect moment for her child to know they were making the right decision. She would synchronise numbers on licence plates and other seemingly inanimate objects within the dreamscape so that her child would feel a sense of connection through the numbers.

Such a miracle was the Great Mother's ability to weave a tapestry of perfection.

But, above all, the Great Mother's greatest delight was to surprise her children. Sometimes, her children would believe that life was predictable. Sometimes her children would move in familiar patterns and habits, where one day meaninglessly rolled into the next. The Great Mother would see that sometimes her children would forget that they too were alive with the same creation energy that birthed them into being. The Great Mother knew all of her children's most sacred dreams and desires. She knew the thoughts that excited her children the most. And so, the Great Mother would bring a miracle to a single moment in time that would make real her children's deepest desires. She would never do it in a way that was predictable or foreseeable. But for each of her children, she orchestrated an infinite number of miracles in absolute alignment with their purest wishes. She asked for nothing in return. But when her children received the miracle and graciously opened their hearts in prayers of gratitude, she would let down her great cosmic lengths of hair and she would wrap the child in an infinitely warm embrace that spoke the silent words—"I will always be here for you."

Chapter Five

I will continue to unfold the tale of the Great Mother and the Eternal Ocean of Light shortly, and as I do, I will weave tales of my own into this journey of shared story. Starting with this one:

When I chose to love myself fiercely, everything changed. When I made courageous choices despite my fears, I was met with more and more love—both within me and all around me.

Change at the beginning takes courage. The first few monumental leaps of faith feel like utter chaos and destruction. At the beginning of great change, it is as though the only way to step out of what no longer serves us is to let the old burn to the ground, leaving nothing behind but ashes. Ashes are easier to walk away from than fully formed empires that feel like dimensional prisons.

In the beginning, following the heart doesn't feel like following the heart. It feels like a path of destruction with no clear insight into where the path will lead. When one has forgotten their soul mission so absolutely, the necessary pivot onto the path of remembering is an agonising one indeed.

When I stood looking out over the empire built upon my inner lies, I looked out upon a dimension birthed from the frequency of untruth. The job that I never really wanted. The house that never truly felt like home. The relationship that never showed me the true meaning of love. A whole tapestry of people, places and things woven together with the thread of my inner lies to self. And the wildest part of it was I never even knew I was lying until I was agonisingly pivoted towards the direction of truth.

A choice presented: stay in one reality—safe, familiar—or let that known reality burn to ashes and leap into a new reality where I had not a single idea of what kind of future was before me. The even deeper truth was that whether or not I chose the old reality, it was already in flames, and I was being guided to jump from a burning building.

Maybe this sounds a little dramatic, but I know that every single person on this Earth has had, is having or will have their burning building moment. But most people live their lives in the agony of a smouldering fire rather than finding the courage to jump.

The jump is a multidimensional leap of faith. The jump is the moment that seals a doorway to the past and all that once was. These moments in life transform our perspectives, how we see the world and how the world mirrors back to us.

In 2018, I jumped from the burning empire I had built. I left my partner, walked away from my home and all my possessions, and I even walked away from my beloved poodle, Jack. The empire was burning, lit by the flame of my inner deception of self. And in my jump, where did I land? On a comfortably soft cushion? No, not quite. I landed in the equivalent of a fast-flowing river with no life vest. After my great jump, I found myself pregnant and in a relationship with a man I barely knew. Tired, moody, nauseous and terrified, I didn't know whether to surrender into some kind of housewife identity and accept an unexpected new fate, or to run entirely—from the new man who was stirring up my deepest inner fears and from my pregnancy.

There is no more rapid shadow work than the acceptance of an unexpected pregnancy in the absence of external stability. Painful questions arose spontaneously from within the depths of my growing womb space. What if he leaves me? How will I cope as a single mother? How will I be a good mother to this baby when I don't even know if I am a good person? A nine-month pregnancy was really just a pressure cooker of the self—an unravelling of my deepest fears of rejection and abandonment. An exposure of the festering wounds of my self-loathing brought forward by my rapidly transforming body. So much was happening inside of me. I was dizzy with emotional turmoil, my mind space wild with a million potentialities for a dire future.

And then: I breathed. I looked up. My man was kneeling before me with an unwavering gaze of utter devotion, and my baby was in my arms.

I had emerged from the cave of a long gestation period where I not only grew a baby but I grieved and let die a version of me that too needed to be burned to ashes. I emerged from a cave that swallowed me into the depths of my own darkness and inner deceptions. The bright light of the sun had been switched on after a nearly year-long winter of the harshest conditions. Suddenly, the light was shining, not just upon me, but from within me. My heart was shining the light of my arrival into the present moment, and in the flick of a dimensional switch, I could see the love that was all around, and I could feel the love that I was.

I birthed my baby and, with her, I birthed myself into a new dimension. I could no longer feel or see the dust of the ashes that held within it the pain I had walked away from. I could only feel and see new life—my new life. A spring garden of truth. Each moment with Scott and baby Lillian was a precious gift that watered the sacred garden I had birthed. Simplicity had arrived at the doorstep of my day, and I was in love—with my family, with life, with the moment. And in overflowing relief of the dawning of a new beginning and absolute gratitude for the sacred miracle that I had been gifted, I looked up to the sky in awe and wonder and I sobbed with tears that whispered, "Thank you. Thank you. Thank you."

Chapter Six

Now, let's delve into the tale of the dreamscape, the Eternal Ocean of Light and the Great Mother. It is a wondrous tale of the power of creation.

Creation began in the effervescent womb of the Great Mother—the one who lovingly brought all things, people, places and beings to life. The energy of creation was like a spark, and the Great Mother was the great spark that exploded everything into being. As she created, the same spark of her love became the innate essence of everything she birthed into being. To the naked eye of the observer of the dreamscape, everything appeared separate and individualised, but in the realm of vibration and frequency, all the Great Mother created was in fact the same—a spark of love in vibrating waveform.

The Great Mother birthed everything into the dreamscape as a pure spark of love. The human souls who had fully remembered their true essence could feel and sense the spark of creation within them, and they could feel and sense that spark of creation mirrored back to them in every other man, woman, child, creature, tree, rock, cloud, flower and blade of grass. This sense of recognition of the spark of creation within all things and within self marked the individualised soul's completion of the full journey of forgetting and remembering the essence of the Eternal Ocean of Light that it truly was. Once the individual soul had mastered the ability to speak, act and live from the fully realised knowing of the spark of light within all things, that soul had realised what was called "oneness", and thus could return to the oneness of the Eternal Ocean of Light at the end of its incarnation with no need to individualise as a soul within the dreamscape again.

On the journey to this embodied realisation of oneness, the human being within the dreamscape needed to be initiated by the journey of life into the remembering of the power of creation it held within. This journey within a single incarnation was the hero's journey—the journey from separate to whole, from powerless to creation, from asleep within the dream to fully realised and awakened to the dreamscape.

The Great Mother guided all her children to ultimately conquer their own journeys within a single incarnation. Whether they followed that guidance depended on their free will.

Each soul's hero's journey was unique—a journey of finding the power of creation within—a journey of uncovering the power of the Great Mother within. Every soul expressed its authentic creative brilliance differently. But pure creative expression, no matter how it appeared in the realm of physicality, was always an expression of the Great Mother and thus an expression of perfection. The soul's hero's journey was guiding them on a path that would lead to the remembering of oneness via unfiltered expression of free-flowing creativity.

You see, creation energy, the energy of the Great Mother, was never separate from or outside of any human soul. The realisation of individual creativity was the human being's gateway to oneness. When one human being realised their power to create freely, they met the aspect of the Great Mother—and indeed the Eternal Ocean of Light—that lived within them.

Human beings were always intended to create. Creation gave them true purpose within the dreamscape, and the path of pure creation was the intended path of the soul in absolute alignment with its sacred mission. And thus, the expressed sacred mission differed vastly from one human soul to another. Creative expression for some human souls was through art, literature, writing and performance. For others, it was through building, architecture and design. Many souls expressed creativity through the bringing together of people, families and communities and through the birthing of shared experiences for all. Some found pure creative expression fulfilled in solitude, and others found it surrounded by people. The path of pure creativity expressed had no limits, but when the Great Mother expressed herself through her children, they always came alive with joy and satisfaction. The intrinsic feelings of joy, satisfaction and aliveness were each human soul's measurable markers for alignment to purpose and alignment to its mission.

The task for the people of the dreamscape to create freely and witness the spark of creation within each other was simple. Yet, complexities arose within the dreamscape that, like a cloud of confusion, prevented the human souls from experiencing their free-flowing creative energy as it was intended.

Each human being could create limitlessly as aspects of the Great Mother. Each human being had a mind that could project images into the dreamscape, and these images could actualise into a holographic reality for that soul and other souls to experience and live within. As a result, there were many realities to experience within the dreamscape, all of which were an illusory hologram, but all the realities felt very real indeed to the human being experiencing them.

The human being would create and experience a reality based upon his or her perception of self. And, each man or woman would have perceptions of self and the world around them based upon their stage of awakening to the dreamscape.

Some human beings who had not met the spark of creation within perceived themselves to be so utterly powerless that they experienced their reality as an invisible cage, a dimensional prison with walls made of their own thoughts and ideas of what life was. Some men and women perceived themselves to be at the mercy of others, victims of life's uncontrollable external circumstances.

Some human beings had met aspects of their ability to create within the illusory system of finance only, and thus lived in a dimensional experience centred around monetary gain. In this dimension, money was creative power. These men and women perceived the human being who had accumulated the most financial wealth to be the most powerful and successful.

There were an infinite number of dimensional experiences to have within the dreamscape, and a human being could flicker from one dimension to another within a single day. The highest and most easeful dimensional experience was the dimension of truth and love. This was the dimension where the human being realised its power to create in absolute alignment with its soul mission. Within this dimension, humanity knew its nature—a spark of the Eternal Ocean of Light. In this dimension, the human being danced through incarnation, enjoying the physical treasures of the dreamscape, knowing that it was indeed a dream. In this dimension, the human being was flickering in wave form, moving in and out of light and physical matter. It was here, dimensionally, that miracles formed within the dreamscape experience. Wonder followed the human being, and beauty serenaded the senses in all moments. This dimensional experience was known as Heaven. And Heaven was such a joy to experience in each moment that the human being knowingly cherished each breath of its incarnation within the dreamscape. The man or woman who had arrived at the dimension of Heaven within the dreamscape knew that, at any moment, a final exhale would free him or her back to the infinite peace and nothingness of the Eternal Ocean of Light, and therefore each breath needed to be honoured as the sacred gift of life it truly was.

Although the dreamscape offered countless dimensional experiences, the loving guidance of the Great Mother was always steering each human soul to widen its perspective of reality and open to its innate creative mastery so that he or she could eventually experience life as Heaven.

Some human souls, who were deeply in the pits of their forgetting the Eternal Ocean of Light they truly were, recognised their power to create even in the absence of love. These human beings, fuelled by ego, separated from their divine mission and engulfed by an insatiable desire to rule and take charge of the dreamscape, came together to unite and amplify their power.

The Great Mother gifted all her children with the ability to create freely. Her children could either create in the name of love, to remember the true essence of who they were and thus enter the dimension of Heaven, or they could choose to create in the name of egoic self-gain, power and greed. Accumulation of power within the dreamscape was like a euphoric drug that fed the ego but separated the human being from the soul. The more separate the human being became from its soul, the more freely it created in the name of egoic power, void of conscience.

An obsession with power within the dreamscape became the destructive focus of a specific group of humans so identified with ego that they became completely void of soul. This group of beings mastered destructive creation. They did not create in the name of love. They hijacked their own spark of creation gifted to them by the Great Mother and formed their own dreamscape dimension with a fixed mission to trap as many souls as possible. This specific dreamscape dimension was the fear-based matrix.

These ego-led beings understood the soul mission, the higher dimension of Heaven and the true loving power of each soul. Despite being void of soul, they had accumulated knowledge of the dreamscape and the true nature of reality, and they used this knowledge to manipulate other human beings into a submissive state that kept them trapped within the fear-based matrix.

The ego-driven beings, void of soul, were no longer being guided by the warm embrace of the Great Mother. Instead, a wicked controlling force intercepted their consciousness, a force not organic to the innate nature of the Eternal Ocean of Light and all birthed from it.

You see, other parallel realms existed alongside the multidimensional dreamscape, although these realms were not visible through the visible light spectrum of human vision. These parallel realms were also illusory dreams, like the Earth dreamscape itself. Alternate realms shaped by completely different creative forces existed at the same time, in the same space as the Earth dreamscape.

Time and space did not truly exist; everything was an aspect of the one, and yet, alternate realms and beings within completely different dreamscapes to Earth were coexisting alongside the Earth dreamscape. Conscious beings with missions separate from the human soul mission were having their own experiences within alternate realms. The only thing that separated human beings from the beings of alternate realms was vibration. Not space, not time, but frequency. So, the alternate realms were inaccessible and unknown to human beings that perceived reality through the limited perspective of Earth's physicality. However, when vibrationally attuned, parallel realms and the beings within them could intercept the Earth dreamscape, and so too could human beings intercept other realms when vibrationally attuned.

Power-obsessed, egoically led humans were fuelled by the desire to entrap as many souls as possible within the fear-based matrix dimension of the Earth dreamscape. When the masses were entrapped into a state of fear-based submission, the power hungry could dominate. This distorted mission of control vibrationally attuned the soulless humans to the alternative realm beings named the Anunnaki. The Anunnaki realm was a realm of decay, evil and fear. The soulless humans became infiltrated by this external controlling force that hijacked their consciousness in order to take control of the Earth dreamscape for themselves. Attuned through resonant frequency, the Anunnaki beings inhabited the bodies and consciousness of the human beings void of a soul so that they were no longer human beings at all, but rather the embodiment of pure evil living within the Earth dreamscape.

And thus, the Earth dreamscape was orchestrated and guided by two opposing forces—the fear-based inorganic Anunnaki and the creative loving essence of the Great Mother and the Eternal Ocean of Light, the organic template to the Earth dreamscape.

The Anunnaki, destructive controllers from a parallel realm, had intercepted the human dreamscape and had their own mission: to inhibit and disrupt the organic soul mission of every human being to exert absolute dominance. The Anunnaki could weave webs of unseen chaos within the multidimensional dreamscape. They hijacked human beings in the highest ranks of power. The Anunnaki mission was carried out through intercepted Earth beings in order to confuse and manipulate the masses. The intercepted soulless Earth beings appeared human to the naked eye, but were not.

The fear-based matrix of the dreamscape became an Anunnaki stronghold—a tightly woven web of finance, politics, government and media where the highest-ranking officials were devoid of human soul and guided by forces of pure evil. The Anunnaki forces orchestrated many aspects of life in the Earth dreamscape—manipulating and tricking the pure hearts of humanity into a life of unconscious submission.

But every single human being that the Anunnaki attempted to entrap and control within the fear-based matrix was still pulsing with the loving mission of their organic original assignment as souls. Every soul, no matter how deep within the control grid, was still being lovingly guided by the Great Mother. The Great Mother would never abandon her children. She even kept a watchful eye over the infiltrated beings hijacked by the Anunnaki, hoping to one day guide them back into resonance with their own human soul.

The organic assignment of each soul as guided by the Great Mother was a force so powerful it could not be matched. But until each soul realised that power within themselves, they would remain trapped by the Anunnaki within the fear-based matrix of the dreamscape.

The realisation of the true divine spark of creation that lived within was the soul's path to freedom.

Chapter Seven

I will get back to the tale of the Anunnaki infiltration within the Earth dreamscape soon. But first, I will share a dimensional experience of my own.

The "golden handcuffs" was what we dubbed it. The golden handcuffs were Scott's ability to earn multiple six figures in a stable job whilst I stayed home and cared for our baby. The golden part was the money and all it enabled. We rented a brand-new suburban home on the outskirts of the Australian city named Perth. The home felt lavish yet sterile. We were paying top dollar in the rental market, and the premium price tag afforded us fancy features not usually present in a standard suburban home—a scullery adjoining the kitchen, a huge master bedroom with a hotel-style spa and a massive garage for our cars and Scott's "boy toys". The "golden" part was never worrying about money.

We named it the "golden handcuffs" because although his job in a senior role in the West Australian gold mines was lucrative, it was a way of life that was agonising to the heart. Scott was bound, and I was trapped in the agony along with him. Working on a mine site in Australia usually means travelling for work within a "fly in, fly out" roster. The FIFO life is what we Aussies call it: big pay packets, massive bonuses and a life where over fifty percent of your time is spent away from your family. This is the "Australian dream". Our new family were stuck in the FIFO Aussie dream—accustomed to the way of life ushered in by big pay cheques.

With my new baby, I was often alone in our big, beautiful, cold home. Life was, of course, "good", but I had become sensitive to the truth of my experience, and I couldn't ignore the lump of melancholy that lived within my throat in most moments of Scott's absence. I was lonely. I would spend one week counting down the nights until Scott's return and the following week holding him close in our bed counting down the nights until he would again leave us. We were prisoners of linear time.

We lived in a suburb called Burns Beach. Our house was a stone's throw from a white-sand beach with gentle waves. We could walk barefoot to the ocean and follow a bike path all the way to a cafe that served great coffee overlooking the water. The whole suburb was brand new; the bird calls of the native bushland bulldozed for a lucrative development were a distant dream. Perfectly curated parks and new trees planted down the centre of freshly tarmacked streets—this was the suburban dream, or in my case, the suburban nightmare.

The house we rented didn't have a garden. It had a small courtyard out the back with a barbeque (of course) and out the front, a small strip of fake grass to ensure an always green look, even in the harshest summer drought. Our neighbour also had fake grass. In fact, most new homes in Burns Beach were freshly landscaped with an evergreen strip of Astroturf. One morning, as I pulled out of the driveway in our SUV, I saw our neighbour vacuuming his lawn as he waved, a friendly smile of good morning. Was I living in *The Truman Show*? Did my neighbours seriously like the fake grass more than normal grass? Did I actually live in a world where the look of green plastic grass had more intrinsic value than the feel of real, living blades that glistened with dew in the morning sunlight?

My life was perfect in the same sense that the fake grass was perfect. From the outside looking in from a distance, all was in order—money, house, baby, husband—check. But I was no longer numb to the insidious festering of untruth within my body. I could smell the stench of illusion when it surrounded me, and I was well aware Scott and I had built a comfortable life that reeked.

Why did people choose to live a life of falsity with fake grass, perfect houses and boring jobs? I could see the answer to this question more clearly than ever, and the answer was rooted in fear. My neighbours were bound to their existence whether they liked it or not because the fear of a life beyond all that was stable and secure kept them prisoner. The fear of the unknown kept them in the safety of the known. The fake grass was the perfect metaphor—of course everyone prefers the texture, smell and look of real green grass but real grass isn't predictable or consistent—it changes, it grows, it dies. We cannot fully control real grass, and so the predictability of fake plastic grass can be a comfortable sacrifice. Some of my neighbours were oblivious to the unacknowledged fear that kept them prisoner. Other neighbours were likely aware of the fear and yet chose complacency. And I have no doubt that a rare few of my neighbours were indeed mirrors of myself—aware of the fear and ready to choose courageous action and change.

I was ready to tear up the fake lawn for the rawness of real weeds.

The moment Scott walked in the door after another agonisingly long week away, I told him, "We can't do this shit anymore." He immediately agreed. That conversation lifted the invisible weight of our intrinsic suffering and paved our way to freedom.

We had changed deeply. We felt different from our neighbours. We were fully alive in a world that, like the fake grass, felt dead. We could feel what was real and what was false, both within our own beings and in our external realities. We had both already spent a number of years committed to our own personal growth and healing, and we had arrived at a stage in our lives where we valued truth and freedom above all else. We were vibrating at a frequency that demanded truth in our reality, even if it was uncomfortable.

It was time to uncuff the golden handcuffs, but the golden handcuffs weren't just gripping our wrists—there was an insidious darkness that had grips of terror within our hearts, our bodies and our minds. We were uncuffing from something real. We were consciously uncuffing from the same grip of fear that I had recognised within my neighbours and their unconscious stuckness. It was as though there was a spell of black magic cast into the psyche of all residents within the entire suburb and beyond. As though an invisible black magic grip of fear was unknowingly terrifying the neighbourhood into a dreamy submission where their homes, cars, jobs and lives were carefully mediated into a vibration of good—too good to change, not worth rocking the boat, comfortably stationary—bound by the invisible grip of fear of the unknown.

The moment we were ready to uncuff the golden handcuffs was the moment I saw it—the handcuffs had imprisoned everyone around me too, but most people were unaware of their stronghold. I saw, I felt and I suddenly deeply recognised a frequency of bondage wearing a mask of middle-class comfortability. It was a nauseating bondage that appeared to serve no one aside from the corporations that each member of my suburban society obediently served through their jobs. I pondered, "Were the corporations of big business casting spells of black magic into society to keep people bound and stuck in their roles as cogs in the machine?" I then realised that Burns Beach was full of CEOs, directors and business owners who were too busy paying their own bills and running their own households to concern themselves with black magic. Indeed, I recognised that the CEOs themselves were under the same spell of bondage and subservience.

What I knew was that Scott, baby Lillian and I were done. We needed to get out. We were ready to walk toward our highest possible potential for our human existence, and that potential did not live within the suburban *Truman Show* nightmare. Despite so much uncertainty, we shared a burning desire to live a life in radically aligned service. We had visions of healing retreats, travel and a home set upon acreage. In shared late-night discussions, we'd explore these visions together and let our limitless imaginations run wild.

But we were stuck at a point of nothingness, terrified to uncuff ourselves to be freed into the deep abyss of the unknown. Where would the money come from? How would we support our child? How would we pay our bills? These were the questions that danced in circles through our minds and conversations. We were terrified, and we did not trust that all would work out well. The only certainty within our being was the certainty that the suburban *Truman Show*, FIFO nightmare we were living was absolutely unendurable for even a moment longer.

With that single certainty, Scott quit his job, we packed our home into a storage unit and we booked three one-way tickets to Bali. Surely the sacred land that brought us together would reveal the next chapter of our journey.

We thrust ourselves into the abyss of the unknown. The golden handcuffs of the suburban nightmare were gone, but the grip of terror that was the fear of the unknown boiled within us more fiercely than ever before.

Our path of unhooking the invisible grips of fear from within and following the expression of our divinely guided creativity was just beginning.

Chapter Eight

Let's continue with the tale of the dreamscape and the souls who navigated it.

The Anunnaki had infiltrated the earthly human dreamscape and were indeed trying to act as a godly force of control with their own destructive agenda. Disguised as human beings, the Anunnaki force sought power in the places where it could best control and manipulate the minds and spirits of all human beings. Absolute power over the physical dreamscape was the goal, and the means of attaining that goal had no limits. Utter evil lived within the humans infiltrated by the Anunnaki force.

Utter evil was never an organic energy true to the earthly dreamscape. The Great Mother created only in the name of love. She created dual forces such as the moon and the sun, woman and man, night and day—but always in the name of love. She orchestrated paths for her human children that on the surface appeared to be chaotic and destructive, but only in the effort for each of her human children to remember the creative spark of love that they truly were. She only created and orchestrated in the name of love.

The Great Mother and the Eternal Ocean of Light witnessed the infiltration of the evil Anunnaki force in the Earth dreamscape and all the death, chaos and turmoil it brought with it. But, the loving guardians and creators of the dreamscape also witnessed a surprising benefit of the Anunnaki infiltration—many human beings were in fact waking up to their innate divinity and love because of the presence of pure evil that surrounded them. In witness of the evil weaving webs of chaos into the dreamscape, the Great Mother and Eternal Ocean of Light chose to allow the presence of the Anunnaki to continue without direct intervention. They recognised the Anunnaki as a catalysing force to assist with the original soul assignment of each human being: to absolutely, fully and completely remember the infinite peace and love that they truly are.

The humans who were fully infiltrated by the Anunnaki force and void of soul made power within the material world their god. We will call these humans the evil ones. The evil ones did not pray to remember love—for love was not a gateway to more material power. Instead they sought to gain as much personal power as possible by syphoning and harvesting the pure life-force essence of every ensouled human being of the dreamscape. The more entrapped within the fear-based matrix a human being became, the more easily its life-force power could be harvested for personal gain. Within the group of the evil ones, there was no love and compassion for one another—no respect nor admiration. Rather, each being was in a race for more personal gain of power, and they would do anything to obtain it.

The evil ones became masters of their dark craft of obtaining more and more power and control within the material world. Although they only harboured hate for one another, the evil ones still recognised their amplified power in coming together with a shared mission of domination. And so the evil ones formed secret groups and congregations where they covertly curated shared plans for the control of the entire dreamscape via the means of discrete and subtle manipulation of the psyche of all human beings within it. Although the evil ones shared their ideas and intentions with each other to master their plans for manipulation, it was important that their agenda remained hidden from the ensouled human beings they planned to entrap. The evil ones knew their plan could only succeed if it existed within the shadows, for once it was exposed for all to see, the ensouled human beings would rise against the manipulation and choose a path to freedom and liberation. Secrecy was imperative to the evil ones above all else.

Over many decades of the linear time illusion within the dreamscape, the evil ones formed a clear hierarchy of power. The secrecy of their plan for absolute dreamscape dominance was best kept within the trusted inner circles of family members. This way, the adults within the high-ranking levels of power could pass their secrets to their children and train their children from birth to reject the organic guidance system of the Great Mother in exchange for power and control. The means of initiating their children were heinous and gruesome, but it was important that the children of the evil ones didn't know love, as love would be the most disruptive force that could crumble and expose their plans for multigenerational dreamscape dominance. So, the evil ones formed a tightly organised inner circle of secrecy spanning multiple generations of just a few families. These bloodlines were the ruling class of the evil ones and rose to the highest levels of power within the physical dreamscape. Members of these bloodlines became the kings and queens of entire empires, the secret heads at the very top of the corporations that owned and conducted all of the dreamscape's illusory economic system. The power of the bloodlines within the physical dreamscape was absolute, and as a result, their ability to manipulate the masses became an easeful game of trickery and deceit that wove through the fabric of all aspects of human reality.

The highest-ranking evil ones would recruit human beings to be the faces and figureheads of different avenues of manipulation. The evil ones would choose the human beings who were gifted with the perfect innate talent to assist with driving their agenda via a certain avenue.

For example, the evil ones knew the power of frequency. The highest-ranking members of the bloodlines held the knowledge of the true nature of reality and knew that the truth of the dreamscape was pure frequency. So, the evil ones focused on manipulating frequency above all else. If the true frequency of the dreamscape as created by the Great Mother was the spark of pure creation birthed through love, the evil ones knew that the frequency of fear would help entrap the souls into the fear-based matrix ensuring that they didn't remember the true nature of love that they actually were.

Fear-based frequency was an imperative factor in the plan of the evil ones. Since human beings absolutely adored music, song and dance, the evil ones infiltrated music as a priority. The evil ones selected singers of remarkable talent to rise to the highest heights of fame and material fortune so long as the singers performed the music curated by the evil ones. Of course, many of the singers selected were having their own inner battle of love versus fear, good versus evil, Great Mother versus Anunnaki. So when the singers were given the opportunity to rise to the greatest heights in the material dreamscape in exchange for the surrender of their true authentic creative expression, they had a choice—to choose the path of the soul or to abandon it. Many divinely guided singers could sense the distortion in the misguided opportunities presented by the evil ones. But many singers chose the path of personal power and gain and were then very susceptible to opening fully to the Anunnaki forces who sought to infiltrate and utilise their talents completely for the fulfilment of the control agenda.

It wasn't just singers the evil ones recruited; it was all types of talented souls who had gifts that could be harnessed to benefit the agenda. Speakers, writers, athletes, academics, leaders—so many gifted souls abandoned their sacred mission in exchange for the gains of personal power they were offered.

Before long, the entire dreamscape was awash with distorted frequency, and it was extremely difficult for the human beings to discern what was true and what was manipulation. The evil ones lured talented beings into the highest ranks of all aspects of human society with the promise of increased personal power and material gain. The purest aspects of human life—such as creativity, music, art, communication, entertainment, food, healing and education—were all completely and totally infiltrated by the force of the Anunnaki. Beautiful, trusting, angelic faces were thrust into stadiums to sing songs designed to enchant and spellbind the masses into a lower frequency. Everything the evil ones created would have a presentation of beauty and allure with an undercurrent of fear and deception: Beautiful singers who sang songs of isolation. Charming politicians who spoke spells of hypnosis. Shiny packaged foods laced with poisons. Luxury family houses for sale with the price tag of a lifetime of bondage. Temptation existed everywhere, and on the surface, all of it seemed well-meaning.

How were the human beings ever going to fulfil their innate mission of remembering the eternal peace and love that they truly were with such deception surrounding them? How were they ever going to wake up to their own innate creative essence when they existed in a reality where that essence was being intentionally syphoned and harvested?

Well, the loving force of the Great Mother and her guidance was unwavering. In fact, it grew more powerful than ever. The Great Mother would not abandon her children. Through the chaos of the web of fear the Anunnaki spun within the dreamscape, the Great Mother's love remained a constant pulse of harmony anchored within the roots of the soil, the waters, the fires and the skies. She never stopped pulsing her love and support through the fabric of the dreamscape. Her children were drowning in a sea of distortion, and she was their life vest. All her children needed to do was feel her support to know that they would never drown. They simply needed to attune to her support to be back in the guiding arms of her unwavering love.

And so, when The Great Mother's children were attuned to her support even slightly, she guided them away from the places within the dreamscape where the fear bondage was holding them tightest. The Great Mother guided her children back to the purest places within the Earth dreamscape. She guided her children out of the fear grid of the cities, back to the rivers, back to the mountains, back to the oceans, back to the forests.

In these natural environments of the dreamscape, there was an audible peace that allowed for the nervous system of the human body to recalibrate back to its organic frequency of love. In the absence of the noise of the cities, the car radios, the televisions and the traffic, the sounds of silence could whisper through the guidance and support of the Great Mother. Nature was the simple antidote to distortion. The bird calls of the forest were the musical symphony of pure harmony the human soul needed to remember its truth. The sound of the running river trickled like a healing massage through the cells of the human body, restoring balance. The roaring waves of the ocean opened the human heart back to love and allowed the tears of separation from the Great Mother to flow.

The plan of the Anunnaki carried out by the evil ones was complex, multilayered and confusing to understand. They designed it to be so. The antidote to their plan and the key to re-attunement back to the Eternal Ocean of Light and the love of the Great Mother was infinitely simple—Be. Here. Now.

Chapter Nine

Thank you for taking this journey with me so far. As I write these tales to share with you, it's funny—it's as though I can feel the essence of the dreamscape holding me within my perceived reality. As I write to share tales of my life in and amongst the tales of the dreamscape, I am led to wonder, am I writing a tale of a fictional dreamscape, or am I indeed within the dreamscape myself writing a true account of the nature of reality? What I know is that I have another story to tell you, about a time in my life when I opened the doorways to Heaven and entered a portal into the infinite.

After Scott and I closed the door on our suburban nightmare and leapt into the unknown, it wasn't exactly happily ever after. But with the certainty within our bodies that told us life would never be the same—there was only one way to look—towards the future. We became unwavering in envisioning the life we longed for. After a short time in the chaos and hustle of Bali, we knew quickly that our longing was for land. We didn't know exactly what we wanted for our futures, but we craved spaciousness and greenery. Our hearts ached to be nestled amongst the trees with the Indian Ocean nearby. Our deepest longings simplified. We longed for self-sufficiency in food—growing vegetables and raising our own chickens for eggs. But for me personally, above all, my heart ached to serve to the fullest capacity of my potential. I had met myself as a healer of others and had accessed a mastery within my psychic abilities that allowed me to know confidently how to move energy, not just within my body but for others as well.

The moment I recognised my innate desire to heal and serve others alongside the divine gifts bestowed upon me, I allowed myself to envision a future where I curated healing retreats and taught others a more limitless way of accessing energy as practitioners. From unlocking my vision for this potentiality and taking baby steps day by day to serve and create in alignment with my spontaneously arising creativity, my life radically transformed into a paradigm of aliveness and aligned service in exactly four years. In a four-year window of rapid inner transformation, I alchemized my fears by following my passions. It was a four-year vortex of up-levelling. An outward quest to birth a healing business that served the masses collided with the necessary purge of my fears, doubts and unresolved layers of unworthiness.

Between the years of 2019 and 2023, I experienced accelerated motion—the birth of another baby, countless house moves, and an exponential unravelling of my inner soul gifts. With each refinement in my vision for a life in service to others, an aspect of me that wasn't ready to embody that vision had to die. So for four years, I died, repeatedly, until I was ready to serve at the fullness of my capacity.

In 2023, the fullness of my capacity to serve and the alignment in my creativity guided me to host a retreat in Bali where I'd train forty-seven beautiful souls in a healing modality I'd birthed called Intuitive Rebirth. I could not believe I'd somehow filled a room with forty-seven highly discerning souls who'd paid to learn a method of healing I'd completely made up, literally out of thin air! Well, as I sat at the front of the yoga space of the resort with forty-seven sets of eyes staring at me waiting for me to say something profound—my mind would flicker to the thoughts of Intuitive Rebirth being based on nothing but psychic insight—no backing, no science, no lineage of mentors. Just little old me writing some big ideas and charging others a substantial amount for the privilege of learning about them. Gulp. At least, that was the perspective of little old me at the time. Little Rhiannon, with barely a couple of qualifications to rub together and certainly no letters after my name. Was I just a giant fraud? I couldn't help but wonder.

But as I sat with the flushing waves of fear that moved through my body whilst the entire room sat in suspended animation watching me, I remembered: All I had done to create this whole modality, event and experience was—allow. I hadn't forced or manipulated myself or others to be there. The experience was born of truth and truth alone. I remembered the hours and days spent connecting to my heart and writing module after module about the purest aspects of divine psychic connection and healing with the power of intention. I remembered the synchronicity and countless chance encounters that had brought me to that moment in time. I was right where I needed to be.

My shadow aspect was a good girl—a high achiever and a people pleaser. But my raw, unfiltered truth has always been a rebel. My purest essence has never taken instruction from others well and has never followed any kind of external blueprint for how to do things. So of course, in my most aligned spark of creativity, I birthed something new. A new way of healing for the rebel who listens to no one but the inner light of divinity that guides and orchestrates all things.

As I sat in the yoga space with the forty-seven eyes glaring at me, I felt the pure essence of my gift as a teacher—the initiator of the sacred rebel who obeys no one but Spirit. And with that silent remembering, I closed my eyes and asked for divine guidance. In a moment of silent prayer and utter devotion, I bowed humbly to the divine orchestrator who had brought me to this incredible point in my life where I had the honour of guiding forty-seven souls into the greatest remembrance of their lives. As I bowed humbly in gratitude, I asked for help. I asked to be shown what to do and how to guide the seven days of intense healing that lay ahead. I had no proper plan. Planning was impossible for me! All I could do was trust.

And so I breathed a few slow, deep breaths into my heart and felt an incredible wave of supporting, loving energy flow through me, the entire room and everyone in it. I guided the group to stand in a circle and to each take the hands of the strangers beside them. When I opened my eyes, this prayer spoke through me: "I call upon Great Spirit. I call upon our highest and brightest guides—benevolent beings of light, angels, ancestors, protector beings. I call upon our guidance system of the highest order." I continued to speak to all the participants in the room from the same connected place of trust, "This week, you will remember who you truly are. You are here to live your most glorious life. Not to bend and break yourself into some distorted mould of society. This week, with the grace of God, all that does not resonate with that truth will be alchemized back to love. *All* of you is welcome here. All your pain, all your pleasure. All your sadness, all your joy. All of your triggers, all of your allowance. I love you. Let's go."

The room filled with a palpable charge of energy. Not just the energy that makes the hairs on your arms stand up but the energy that shifts dimensions. We had entered another realm, and it was a realm where miracles would happen. And happen they did.

By day five of the retreat, we'd moved into a dreamlike realm of healing and love that made the days and nights merge into one. Everyone's deepest fears, traumas and hidden shadows were being exposed by the transparency of pure, palpable love. Earth-shaking fear would bubble up within one participant at a time, so strong it was as though the fear would suffocate and consume them—all so that the fear could be felt and loved. Hidden, long forgotten memories of childhood trauma would surface in some participants, and as they accessed and released the pain of these stored traumas, purge buckets would be filled. So deep was their letting go.

It was a big and radically exhausting week in the depths of healing. But I was in awe of the divine orchestration of the entire thing. Every day and night I would pray for utter support and help. During the moments where I felt I had met my edge in what I could facilitate and hold, I would close my eyes and pray for help, and like magic, I'd receive a sudden down-pouring of near instantaneous life-force vitality and clarity.

It was on day five that something extraordinary happened. One participant had already experienced a huge week of healing. She'd cried, screamed and purged to the depths of her soul but there was something that still lingered. She was a beautiful woman with a soft heart, but when I addressed the group, it was as though her gaze was not her own. Her soft, loving eyes would shapeshift into hateful sneer and then flash back to softness. I had worked with entities before in the psychic realms, but I had never experienced such an obvious infiltration of someone's true essence as what I saw within her. The entity inhabited her body, and it was plain to see for anyone with eyes to notice. The higher the energy of the retreat centre became through the frequency of pure love, the more exposed the entity living within the woman was.

The entity was right there in the room with us.

During the partnered healing for that day, the beautiful woman accessed the shame she was carrying within her body for the decisions she'd made in her past. She cried huge sobs of sadness for herself and let out whimpers of despair as she felt the contraction of the sexual violation of her past surface. Her partner and I guided her to feel each wave of contraction within her emotional body and to continue to give it a sound of release. And so whimpers, cries and screams of hurt kept flowing from her body as she went deeper and deeper into the inner realms of herself. As she journeyed deeper within her own body and explored the uncharted realms of her being, something changed. The entity revealed itself, and this time its presence lingered. If you've ever seen *The Exorcist*, this was that. The beautiful woman was no longer present, it seemed, just the face of a laughing joker finding all the attention very satisfying indeed. The energy changed from that of love to that of the most vile, sickening predator in all of humanity. Her tongue flickered side to side, and her hips ground in circles as though the entity was receiving some kind of sexual gratification from dwelling in her body.

I did everything I knew to do as a psychic healer, but the entity wasn't leaving. It was beyond anything I'd ever experienced. To call it an entity was an understatement. It was a fully embodied demon. Pure evil embodied in a divine soul.

I must admit, for a moment I was afraid. But this was my show—my retreat. I had organised this whole bloody thing, and this was happening under my direction! That situation caused me to do the only thing I knew how. I closed my eyes; I prayed and asked for help. The voice inside spoke clearly, "The demon thinks it's powerful and big because you're so close to it. Move back." I acted on the directions and did as guided immediately. With my gaze fixed on the demon, I sauntered backward towards the room's far end. Suddenly, the demon looked like a little squirming blob of black goop. I could see the entity clearly from the back of the room. It wasn't powerful; it was afraid. The entity was fear—terrified. I could see that this demon was just the manifestation of generational terror from heinous abuse, and I knew that where there is fear, there can be no power.

Once I saw the true powerlessness of this fear-based entity, I spoke out loud to the demon as I gazed into the depths of its distortion, "I. SEE. YOU." And with that, the beautiful woman collapsed into sweet sobs of relief. Her eyes opened, soft. She was home in her body, and the entity was gone. I closed my eyes once more to confirm, "Is it gone?" I asked my guidance system. "It's gone," my inner voice of clarity replied.

The powerful healers held the beautiful woman in their warm embrace and spent the next hour in utter devotion to her, just as the Great Mother would. This woman gifted me with an experience I am forever grateful for. She showed me that there is nothing to fear because love is the most powerful force in all existence. The beautiful woman taught me that there is no power where there is fear and therefore there is nothing to fear in all the universe. We are love, and love alchemizes all things.

Chapter Ten

Back in the tale of the dreamscape, another fear-based frequency was wreaking havoc through the minds and bodies of humanity.

The Anunnaki carried out a reign of terror within the fear-based matrix of the dreamscape, and their power depended on the secrecy of their existence. Divine souls living within the fear-based matrix would perceive themselves to have absolute autonomy over their lives and their ability to decide. However, the souls within the fear-based matrix made all decisions based on fear, not from their innate wisdom of love, thus trapping them unknowingly in a self-perpetuating prison constructed by their own unconscious fear.

The power system in the fear-based matrix was money—an illusory economic system of no true value. The evil ones ruled over the masses through this illusory system of control, and the souls entrapped within the matrix would unconsciously make all decisions based upon deep-rooted fears attached to this system. Divine souls would quash all innate creative talents and willingly give their life-force power to tasks performed day in, day out for a system of money credits received as digital numbers observed via a personal screen device.

The men and women of the fear-based matrix within the dreamscape would observe the rise and fall of the digital numbers on the screen, and a distorted emotional trigger of either lack or abundance would activate within their bodies. When the digital number went down, the souls ruled by fear would contract emotionally and energetically. Since all food, water, and shelter were purchased through an exchange system based upon the digital numbers, questions about their basic survival would arise.

Those souls in the fear-based matrix had deeply forgotten how the Great Mother provided for them; they perceived the digital numbers to be the only source of reliable provision. If the numbers went to nothing, they perceived, destitution would set in—hunger, loss, homelessness. In the fear-based matrix this was all possible when the numbers went to zero. And so, onward with the tasks performed day in, day out. Onward with the living arrangements and relationships that brought a sense of predictability to the safety triggered by the numbers on the screen. Onward with the lack of inspiration and loss of joy, since a life committed to the accumulation of the numbers on the screen was of top priority.

The unconscious fear of losing the numbers on the screen ruled the souls imprisoned in the fear-based matrix, thus allowing it to exist. All the jobs fulfilled by the souls for digital credits were necessary tasks that needed to be completed to uphold the fabric of the fear-based matrix society.

Government control systems, banking, entertainment and media, education, construction and more—there were an infinite number of tasks that needed to be carried out in order to uphold a society that on the surface looked like beauty and freedom, but at the depths was nothing more than a mirage of deception orchestrated through fear.

Some souls never entered the fear-based matrix of the dreamscape. They were born as babies into loving homes and held at the breast of mothers who radiated the same unconditional qualities of the Great Mother herself. Some souls would incarnate at the last stages of their journey of remembering the eternal peace and presence they truly were and thus would navigate their life with the expansive true perception of reality, immune to the fear-based control mechanisms of the Anunnaki.

For other souls, they would only wake up to the truth of their own nature and the nature of reality through feeling the distortion of the fear-based matrix. For some, the fear-based matrix was the catalyst to begin their journey of remembering.

In order to become imprisoned within the fear-based matrix, they would need to become imprisoned by their own mind and the lies perpetuated on themselves through perceptions of reality based upon fear. There were no bars keeping the souls imprisoned, and thus the bars were of their own making—a construct of the mind built upon fear. When there was no fear, there was no imprisonment, and the soul would leave the fear-based matrix and exist in a higher dimensional reality within the dreamscape—closer to Heaven.

Thus, the Great Mother would guide and orchestrate experiences for the entrapped souls to face their fears, feel them and transform them into courageous love. Through this alchemy, souls found their power and reconnected with the essence of self, the Eternal Ocean of Light. This essence of self was so infinite that nothing could imprison it.

And so fear was the most powerful catalyst for the alchemy of remembering available to the souls within the dreamscape. Fear was the ember for the fires of transformation within the men and women of the dreamscape.

The question was: Would the fear of an experience swallow up the soul and suck the soul into a self-perpetuating prison of the matrix? Or would the fear catalyse the alchemy of true remembering? That was for each soul to decide, as they navigated every aspect of the multidimensional dreamscape through their own free will.

The power of the Anunnaki depended on the souls remaining trapped through unconscious fear. Unconscious fear did not catalyse the alchemy of remembering in the same way that conscious palpable fear did. Unconscious fear festered in the subtle realms of the unconscious mind, creating a distorted reality that was perceived and experienced as the truth. This is where the Anunnaki aimed to keep their enslaved masses. For fear to remain unconscious within the souls, it needed to be triggered by a traumatic experience, fed through distorted frequency, and then suppressed into the unconscious mind and body through numbing and sedation. And thus, there were three separate techniques used to keep the enslaved masses in an unconscious fear state—trauma, frequency warfare and sedation.

A multigenerational erosion of human empathy wove trauma into the fabric of the fear-based matrix. The natural loving quality of empathy made it impossible for one human being to harm another. Love and kindness were the innate blueprint of the soul as aspects of the Great Mother. And so, the erosion of human empathy was necessary in order for one man or woman to inflict hurt on another. The Anunnaki ruled through secrecy, and thus the orchestration of trauma would need to be between the human beings, not directly and obviously from the evil ones themselves.

Multiple avenues facilitated systematic empathy erosion. Entertainment such as movies played via big black screens would show violent, bloody murder and horrific acts of abuse in a glorified and sometimes even humorous manner. Other entertainment aimed at the male populace, again through personal screen devices, would show heinous acts of sexual violence performed against women. The fear-based matrix normalized and encouraged people to watch such horrors via screens as entertainment, which eroded empathy.

They fed a variety of poisonous beverages named alcohol into the populace to suit all tastes. Alcohol would separate the soul from the body and make it easy for Anunnaki infiltration. The fear-based matrix encouraged and glamorised drinking alcohol. Alcohol was a huge part of all aspects of social interaction, and people rarely omitted it from gatherings outside of work. Alcohol and the feeling it induced had an addictive quality and became a crutch for many men and women within the fear-based matrix.

With innate empathy subtly eroded and alcohol within the body, the Anunnaki could move through a human being to carry out atrocious acts of hurt and violence upon another. These traumatic events would have lasting imprints on both the victim and the perpetrator. The traumatic event caused negative emotions like shame, grief, anger and terror to imprint within the body, locking the person into a lower frequency that drastically distorted their thoughts and perceptions of themselves and the world. From this distorted perception of reality, the traumatised person would manifest a reality based upon that trauma—attracting more situations and experiences that triggered the same unresolved shame, grief, anger and terror. It was also very easy for traumatised people to traumatise others, since they were acting from a frequency of unresolved anger and fear.

When many souls within the fear-based dreamscape experienced trauma, they could easily perpetuate multigenerational cycles of trauma.

Frequency warfare was also carried out by the evil ones to perpetuate fear in subtle ways. The evil ones sent hypnotic waveforms into the masses to fuel fear. The evil ones sent electromagnetic radiation tuned to fear frequencies into households, and every household's black screen personal devices received it. Giant cell-phone towers dotted around cities and towns, and gargantuan frequency stations situated remotely could send out waves of fear unknowingly through the populace. They purposefully tuned the fear frequency into music and all other forms of entertainment. They also wove low frequencies into mass-produced food, water and medicine using chemical poisons. The Anunnaki control system covered all avenues.

With the masses largely traumatised and controlled through fear frequency, it became very important to the Anunnaki that the souls didn't use their own free will to alchemize their fear into courageous love and set themselves free from the matrix. And so, sedation was an imperative aspect of the control system of the fear-based matrix. Where one could not feel and attune to their own fear and trauma, one could not let the spark of its embers catalyse their remembering. Sedation of the masses was imperative to the evil ones. Therefore, they built the entire reality and way of life for the souls within the fear-based matrix upon not feeling—not feeling what is alive within the body, not feeling what is present in the surrounding reality.

To create a reality of non-feeling, the evil ones destroyed nature, clearing the way for concrete jungles with sharp lines and inorganic materials. They pumped drugs into the masses, disguising them as healthcare and entertainment. These chemical compounds made it nearly impossible for human beings to feel their authentic internal emotional processes and created confusion and detachment from the spark of truth that lived within. Human beings could escape into addictive forms of entertainment and distorted virtual realities on personal screen devices when their own inner reality became uncomfortable. All of this was intentional sedation. They purposefully numbed the masses to their own pain and fear. Their controllers intentionally suspended them in obliviousness because it kept them from recognizing their fear and trauma, which would have set them free.

From this orchestrated, distorted obliviousness, the trauma and fear bubbled within. And every soul, with the innate power of free will, could choose—a more comfortable sedation or the courageous path of feeling that would set them free.

The Great Mother never stopped trying to guide her children toward the dimensional experience of Heaven—the dimension wherein they know themselves as sparks of creation, aspects of the Eternal Ocean of Light. And so for each of her children trapped within the fear-based matrix, she simply guided them to the places, people and experiences that reminded them of how to feel all that was authentically alive within the depths of their own bodies. She guided them away from the screens. She led them back to nature. She steered them away from alcohol, drugs and numbing forms of entertainment. And the Great Mother guided her children to feel and heal all the hidden fears and traumas they had been denying within themselves.

For those deeply entrapped within the fear-based matrix, making the courageous decision to choose to feel instead of sedate always brought with it its own fears. The entrapped held not only their own traumas within their bodies but also the traumas of their ancestry, every soul incarnation, and the entire human family because they were, in truth, one.

The more an entrapped soul leant into the courage to feel and heal its suppressed fear and trauma, the more free the soul became to navigate the multidimensional dreamscape with complete awareness. This freedom that came from feeling and alchemizing fear rendered the Anunnaki control systems powerless.

Feeling and healing were the gateway to freedom. Feeling and healing, en masse, was the pathway to destroying the fear-based matrix and the Anunnaki infiltration within the dreamscape.

The more a man or woman felt and transmuted their own trauma and fear, the clearer their perspective of the true nature of reality became. Through deep and absolute inner alchemy, the lens of truth clarified, and true vision of the previously unseen realms became possible. The healed and awakened soul within the dreamscape could see, through closed or opened eyes, the energy of the Anunnaki and where it had woven itself into so many aspects of society and people. Through the lens of truth, the awakened soul could see the true nature of the Anunnaki—fear, simply. From the perspective of true seeing, the awakened soul could expose the distorted control system that exists only in secret, revealing it fully and destroying its power with one sentence spoken through a heart of courageous love: I SEE YOU.

Chapter Eleven

The interconnectedness between my life and the tale of the dreamscape appears now absolute. If the tale of the dreamscape is actually the true story of the nature of reality, then suddenly it feels that I have spent my whole life in some kind of energetic preparation for the role I play in destroying the Anunnaki infiltration here on Earth. I have felt the strong grip of the fear-based matrix as a noose around my neck in many chapters of my life. I have numbed myself into an oblivious sedation through drugs and alcohol to avoid my darkest fears. And a path guided me to meet my inner demons, so that I could transmute them and set myself free. Now I guide others to do the same for themselves.

Everywhere I look—at supermarket checkouts, at petrol station pumps and on crosswalks—I can see demonic infiltration within the faces of the teenagers, grandmothers and sons coexisting with me in my local community. I am living in a multidimensional reality with different dimensions intersecting one another in every moment. One minute I am buying groceries for my children's packed lunches, the next I am witnessing the powerful hold of Anunnaki infiltration through the mother who stands beside me, trembling with unprocessed rage as she snaps at her disobedient child.

The more I surrender to the truth of my body and my heart, the more deeply I see the truth of all that surrounds me. As I feel the layers of unprocessed fear and grief stored within the eternal inner fabric of my being, the more anchored in a state of love I become. In love, I am. In love, I remember. In love, I am home. In love, I am free.

And yet, how easy it has been for me to forget these simple truths.

Ever since Scott and I took the leap of faith to turn our backs on the fear-based matrix that had gripped us in the suburban nightmare, we have been listening to the whispers of guidance ever so quietly showing us the way. Signs and messages from the Divine have illuminated a path, and despite our recurring surfacing doubts, we have followed them.

We have sold businesses, sold our family home, invested heavily in our creative endeavours, walked away from jobs, moved country—you name it. If it felt right, we listened, despite the fears. And as a result, little by little, our life has become more spectacular. The guidance has come in many forms, but most often it has come through a feeling experienced as a visceral inner knowing. Although I would now consider myself to be deeply psychic, when making major life decisions, the most laser-sharp messages have always reached me in my gut knowing rather than my psychic vision. When I knew we needed to sell our house, the idea of remaining in the house suddenly felt nauseating—like the house itself would engulf me. I suppose when I met Scott and was guided to leave my ex, the old relationship nauseated me with the same engulfing quality. This has been my marker for key decision-making confidence.

If I weren't to listen to the discomfort within my body urging me to make a change, what would happen? Well, I have noticed in those closest to me that truth unexpressed over long periods of time manifests as disease. Perhaps you've noticed this within yourself or someone around you? When we lie to ourselves, it is out of the fear of expression of our truth. When we reject the wisdom of our bodies demanding change, it is because of the fear such change invokes—the fear of stepping up into a new opportunity or of cutting ties from an expired identity. Fear of expressing and acting upon visceral truth within is what keeps us stuck in rigid realities that no longer serve our expansion. When we do not create a change in our outer reality by stepping into the fire of our fear, we cannot alchemize such fear and elevate into a higher dimension of greater love. Truth expresses love, and our bodies show us what is true—whether we like such truth or not.

I notice that the guidance system surrounding me turns up a notch when I somehow ignore the visceral knowing moving through me. It's like the divine orchestrator of this incredible reality will find any means necessary to stop me from taking the wrong path. First, I get a sign that is equivalent to the gentle tickle of a light feather that whispers, "Go this way, Rhiannon." And then if I ignore the feather for long enough, I get the energetic equivalent of a big slap around the face.

In 2024, Scott and I lived back in Bali with our then five- and three-year-old daughters. We were hosting five retreats in one year, training practitioners in the intuitively based trauma healing modality we created, Intuitive Rebirth. We had big visions for the future ahead and were spending each day playing in a childlike state of creativity and wondrous imagination. Scott and I would sit on beanbags next to the pool of our villa watching the fireflies dance around us each evening once the kids were in bed. We'd order in raw desserts from a local vegan cafe and get lost in conversations about the life we wanted to create. We could see it so clearly: a retreat centre, permaculture gardens with a food forest and profoundly meaningful healing work connected to the land. As we wove our visions together, speaking over one another with overflowing excitement, we knew one thing was for sure: Together, we were a powerful force of creation.

During the day, I would search Bali property sites for boutique hotels that would fit the vision. Very few properties were financially within our reach but one caught our attention. It was an eleven-bedroom, three-star hotel with a purpose-built yoga temple and beautiful gardens. The hotel was situated remotely on Bali's east coast, relatively unaffected by the relentless expansion of Bali's concentrated development. I contacted the owner of the property and organised a visit straight away.

A couple of days later, we ordered a taxi, and it drove us almost three hours to the foothills of the Karangasem mountain region, where Wayan, the hotel manager, greeted us with a nervous smile. Wayan welcomed us like royalty. There were no other guests staying in the hotel, and for our arrival, the staff all but rolled out the red carpet. The porters set our bags down in the lobby, which also served as the hotel restaurant. From the outside balcony of the restaurant, panoramic views of the distant ocean glistened over the tops of the banana and frangipani trees of the garden below. It felt like we'd arrived at a hidden gem—a paradise for our taking.

The experience upon arrival at the hotel was without fault. Immediately, Wayan toured us around the grounds and the rooms; despite the age and dust of each space, we could see the potential to bring our vision to life.

As we wandered through the grounds casually inspecting each bedroom, Wayan revealed insights into the inner workings of the business operations. The more Scott's lighthearted Australian humour and manner created ease within the dynamic, the more Wayan's tongue loosened. Trickles of information about the staffing, finances and sustainability of the business itself flowed, and within my body, inner alarm bells sounded gently. And then I would look around at the beauty—ahhh, it was so stunning, I told myself, and within our price range too!

As the grounds tour stopped at the yoga space nestled on the edge of a flowing creek, a powerful sound echoed through a speaker in the distance, startling me and cutting through the hum of the cicadas in the surrounding jungle. It was the bellowing echo of the call to prayer from the neighbouring mosque, as loud as a car CD player turned to full volume. The sound overshadowed all else, and conversations paused, suspended mid-sentence whilst we all waited patiently for the prayer to end. There was an enchanting quality to the song blasting from the mosque and, although it startled my nervous system from the sheer volume of the speaker and its sudden onset, it was easy to feel the beauty of the melding of religions within the town and the power of the prayer itself. And yet, my body felt uneasy.

"Where is the mosque?" I asked Wayan.

"Just over the creek," he replied nervously, sensing my uncertainty. I contemplated inwardly, perhaps the call to prayer would sound beautiful weaving through our retreat space? Or perhaps it'd be jarring to the nervous system of the participants when in a deep state of trance and healing, as it was to mine? I was performing the inner mental gymnastics of talking myself into the perfection of the mosque neighbours and their five-times-daily song. It was Bali after all, I told myself, a melting pot of traffic sounds, dogs barking, Hindu culture colliding with Muslim culture in total harmony and respect. Could I not open into absolute acceptance and allowing, since I am, after all, the outsider? Was the jarring of my nervous system actually my own unconscious intolerance and judgement? Perhaps I just need to open and surrender into more compassion and acceptance?

That night, the four of us settled into the premium villa suite, the best room the resort offered. The room was cosy and generously sized. They furnished the room with white rattan armchairs and traditional white wooden window shutters. There was an old-world European charm to the room, with the energy of Bali etched into the wood carving of the timber joglo-style cabin. After late-night conversations in bed exploring the possibilities of the resort and dreaming up potential renovations and opportunities for expansion, Scott and I fell into a peaceful sleep. Suddenly we woke up with a jarring start. The call to prayer. It seemed even louder than the evening before. "What time is it?" I asked Scott.

"4:15 a.m.," he replied, reaching over to check his phone.

"Oh my goodness, this could be a problem."

After the song had ended, we both fell back into a deep morning sleep. When we awoke with the birds chirping and the morning sunlight streaming through the shuttered windows, it was as though we had completely forgotten about the unrequested wake-up call.

That day, we enjoyed everything the hotel offered—the beautiful pool, the manicured tropical gardens, the warmth of the staff and the two hotel cats. The staff were beginning to feel like family. The more time we spent with them, the more we learnt of their families and their struggles. Because of the obvious poverty in the neighbouring village, a desire to help overwhelmed our retreat centre vision and settled heavily on our hearts. Wayan shared of the financial strain the business had experienced and how each staff member had sacrificed a huge portion of their salary in order to keep the hotel from absolute closure. The staff were working for around $100 USD per month and could barely feed their families from what they were making. Wayan told us the staff were reluctant to search for other jobs since opportunities were scarce in their small village, and proximity to family and the village temple was what they valued above all else. As well as acting as the hotel manager, Wayan was also the leader of the Hindu village temple—he was holding the weight of the entire village on his shoulders and it showed in the strain of his smile and the red veins in his eyes. Scott and I suddenly felt an overwhelming sense of responsibility for the hotel and its staff. The foreign owners were nowhere to be seen, and the Balinese staff seemed to be drowning in the burden of their own destitution whilst upholding a shiny facade of positivity to win us over—their potential financial saviours.

There was a huge, energetic projection of desperation emanating from each staff member as they fussed over our stay and every aspect of it. They even helped us with the kids whenever they could.

When we left the hotel and arrived back at the villa we called home, it was decision time. Let's just go for it, we decided! It felt like a once in a lifetime opportunity to purchase a hotel within our price range and bring a vision into absolute fruition on a timeline much faster than we ever imagined possible. Yes, the finances of the business itself were terrible, but we had a different business model. It was the property itself we were buying, not the failing three-star hotel business.

We wasted no time in engaging Australian lawyers specialised in Balinese property acquisition and began the costly and arduous process of negotiating a price and drawing up the contracts for the sale.

During the tedious weeks of the negotiation process with the European-based property owners and our lawyers, I received an online Vedic astrology session. I had booked it a few weeks prior with Drew, the Godfather of Astrology, as my best friend, Abby, had described him. Drew was incredible—beyond knowledgeable in the science of Vedic astrology, I realised within minutes of the session that he was a psychic too—a mystic with innate gifts of knowing. The session blew my mind. From my birth time and day, he read insight from my birth chart and detailed aspects of my character and unique essence that felt so precise, I couldn't have described myself better. At the end of the session, Drew asked if I had questions for him. I told him about the hotel and our plans to transform it into a healing retreat centre. Drew asked me for its location and for more specific details in order to ascertain a reading on its viability and alignment for me on my highest path. He spent a few minutes in silence, calculating and then closing his eyes, preparing his answer for me.

"The property has a lien on it," he concluded with certainty. "Research the property more before you buy it." Wow. That's specific, I thought.

Still, despite what Drew had warned, Scott and I proceeded with the negotiations. During one series of email correspondence with the owners, they revealed a legal case against the property and followed up by ensuring us it was of no consequence to us and wouldn't affect our ability to safely and successfully purchase the property. Drew was right! We discussed the legal case with our lawyer, and she warned us not to go ahead, describing the property as a red-flag property.

Yet, the feeling of responsibility for the staff and the village continued to pull at our hearts. Scott and I continued to fantasize about how we would transform the yoga space with a new bamboo roof and turn the restaurant into a Zen den of colourful floor cushions where guests would be served healthy elixirs and ceremonial cacao. We talked about how we would buy food supplies to give to the staff and maintain a storage room filled with rice, fresh vegetables, and household items that they could take home whenever needed. We were excited to reimburse every staff member for all losses incurred and to replace all hotel furniture, donating existing beds, bedding, towels and couches to the villagers since many slept simply on the bare floor.

We had become fixated on a vision that we wouldn't let subside, despite the glaringly obvious signs telling us to walk away—the mosque, Drew, the lawyer. Why weren't we seeing the signs? Even the feeling within our bodies wasn't that of excitement. It was that of responsibility and duty to the staff and the villagers. We were attuned to the essence of humanitarianism, which would bring a sense of reward from our overflowing acts of generosity and kindness. But we had lost the true essence of our original vision. We were being guided by the fear of letting the staff down. We were acting from a sense of obligation fuelled by our own fear of disappointment. On reflection, there was a fear that if we didn't buy this hotel, there would never be another within our price range. It was now or never, the distortion whispered.

Twenty thousand dollars deeper in legal fees and business visas, we still hadn't signed a contract. However, we had been negotiating for months, and after a couple more hotel visits, we became deeply emotionally entangled with every staff member as we uncovered more stories of poverty and struggle.

One day, on the daily journey home from collecting Lillian and Awen from their Montessori kindergarten, I experienced a universal slap in the face because I had ignored all the feather tickles. As a family, we travelled everywhere by scooter. Scott would drive, our five-year-old Lillian would stand in front of him, hands resting in the middle of the handle bars, and I would balance on the back with little Awen tucked in my lap. We knew it was dangerous, but with car traffic at a near constant standstill, family scooter transport was a Bali way of life—for locals and expats alike. As we turned the corner into our neighbourhood village, onto a road we drove upon multiple times per day, an unexpected force collided with the front of my right shin, thrusting me off the back of the scooter and bouncing me on my tailbone multiple times, leaving me in a stupefied state, confused and numb, in the centre of the tarmacked road.

After a moment of complete loss of vision and everything going blank, I started to recover a blurred focus and a ringing in my ears set in. I looked up at the scooter twenty or thirty meters up ahead and saw my whole little family—Scott, Lillian and Awen, somehow all perfectly fine—staring back and me on the ground. A local man with a food vendor setup affixed to the back of his motorbike had swerved into our lane whilst overtaking, and his steel food cart had collided with my right knee and leg, shunting me off the bike with force.

I was numb and in absolute shock. Scott rushed over to help me off the road, and we sat together on the kerb with his arm wrapped around me. I was in disbelief. Thank God the children were okay! I was spellbound. How on Earth did little Awen, who was resting asleep upon my lap somehow come out of the collision completely unscathed? How did she manage to remain on the bike when the lap she was sleeping on was thrust off? Once I had found some composure, the four of us nervously clambered back onto the bike, and with the trepidation of first-timers, we set off on the very short drive back to the villa.

When we arrived home, the pain set in. My hips were in agony. I cautiously peeled off my skirt and underwear and gasped with the sharp sting of the raw flesh that had been grazed from my buttocks. My butt was red raw with huge grazes down one side of my hip. My tailbone felt broken, and the impact site at my ankle, knee and shin had deep cuts, bruises and flesh wounds. The tension of the suspended shock, which had given me the energy to get me out of danger, softened, and I sobbed deeply as I curled into a foetal position on my bed in tender agony. I lay in bed for hours, sobbing and feeling the pain and shock of what had happened. And yet, despite the pain, I knew I was okay. Upon deeper assessment as the hours passed, my tailbone injury was not as bad as it initially seemed. I could walk. I could move all of my limbs and spine fully. The major injuries were nothing more than severe bruising and grazes to the skin. It was a miracle, I realised. And the most beautiful aspect of the miracle was that my children were completely unharmed and seemingly rather unfazed by the entire incident.

The trauma of the accident stayed in my body, locked and fixed, for a couple of weeks. It became hard for me to access free-flowing tears, and I felt disconnected from Spirit—unable to channel and connect psychically in the way I normally would.

So I booked a session with an intuitive osteopath. I knew I needed someone with wisdom of the physical body and the psychic attunement to hold me emotionally. Phil, the osteopath in Ubud, was exactly that. I went to his clinic set in his villa in the middle of a rice paddy, and he wove an attuned magic of massage and spinal manipulation through my body that triggered waves of strong emotional release. He guided me to breathe deeply into the spaces he touched. With my inhale, he would press and with my exhale, I would release tears and screams of letting go. My body was unravelling. The tension and the trauma were releasing as I felt it, breathed with it, and allowed the sound of its free-flowing truth to leave with my raw expression. Visions opened in my mind's eye. Visions of flowers and gardens bloomed from my reopening heart. I had visions of my late grandmother's pain that she too had carried in her hips and pelvis from childbirth, and I released her uncried tears through my own. I had visions of an expansive land back home in Australia and a simple life of freedom. As I felt the agonising pain of my tailbone with each point Phil touched, I accessed a homesickness that I hadn't acknowledged and a longing to return to Wadandi Boodja—where the kookaburras sang and the kangaroos roamed. Phil brought me home—home to my body. And home to truth.

When I got home to Scott, it was an instant knowing—"We are not buying that fucking retreat centre. And, we're going home."

Trauma freed me from a wrong decision that would have altered the course of my life drastically. Trauma was the re-pivot when I had forgotten how to listen to the subtleties. Trauma invited me to access my body so that I could unravel the deeper fears that attuned me to a misaligned path.

Indeed, trauma initiates us and frees us if we allow it to. Events of monumental suffering have the power to bring to the surface all buried untruths that we have carried within. Events that challenge us are capable of transforming us if we do not numb ourselves to the intensity of that power as it bubbles within.

When invited to, the intensity of suppressed trauma rises up through the body like a caged lion breaking itself free—shattering false perceptions, lifting veils and breaking all illusions.

Chapter Twelve

Now, let's delve back into the tale of the dreamscape.

The Anunnaki had infiltrated all aspects of life within the physical reality of the dreamscape; however, they could never truly rule the dreamscape since there was indeed nothing to rule. The dreamscape was an illusion—a multidimensional mirage of perception unique to each soul who navigated it. The dreamscape was birthed from love by the Great Mother, and a pulse of simple truth reverberated through all facets of life, since life itself was simply the Eternal Ocean of Light having an experience of forgetting and remembering its true nature.

For the soul with true vision, the dreamscape was a paradise of experience. It was alive with spectacular beauty. The bird life chorused through the trees in a symphony with the sounds of children playing in open fields. Sunlight danced on each flowing wave, as the ocean waters glistened with a million stars of their own infinite nature. The dreamscape transformed with the seasons, awash with new beauty and colour at each turn of the cyclical wheel of the calendar. Autumn reds and oranges, settled into a desert of winter white. Spring brought with it the perfume of lilacs and the buzzing of bees as they settled onto wild yellow flowers. And the intensity of the summer sun brought to full bloom vine-ripened medleys of juicy tomatoes, succulent and bursting with vitality. Abundance was the ever-present truth of the dreamscape since the Great Mother only birthed abundantly.

All one ever had to do to free themselves from the grips of the fear-based matrix was to open their eyes to the organic beauty that surrounded them. The truth of the dreamscape was beauty, and observing this organic beauty harmonised all distortion. The Great Mother loved her children deeply, and although she watched on as they suffered at the hands of evil woven through the dreamscape by the Anunnaki, she knew in her eternal wisdom, as an aspect of the Eternal Ocean of Light, that all of her children were right where they needed to be in their journey of remembering.

The Great Mother was a master creator; indeed, she was creation. She had birthed the dreamscape into being, and because the Anunnaki wasn't organic to her creation, she knew that all souls within the dreamscape held infinitely more power than the Anunnaki. The souls were, in their pure essence, love. And love was the most powerful energy within the dreamscape. The Great Mother watched on as her children suffered at the hands of the Anunnaki, but she knew all that was required of them to destroy the Anunnaki was simply to remember their power as aspects of loving creation. From a parallel realm, the Anunnaki had intercepted the dreamscape. They originated in an anti-life realm as inorganic beings, and they were formed through a process of anti-life matter multiplication. The Anunnaki, infused with the essence of anti-life distortion, held powers that didn't resonate with the organic nature of the dreamscape and thus, in reality, their powers were actually redundant.

The Great Mother knew this truth, and thus she held no fear for the Anunnaki infiltration. She knew that, in an instant, the power of her love could destroy them. So, better still, she used their presence within the dreamscape to assist the souls in their journey of remembering. As she watched on as men and women infiltrated by evil perpetuated violence and harm against one another, she sent waves of support and guidance to illuminate doorways of escape, pathways of healing, and routes of disentanglement from distortion. She was always present for every one of her children, but she knew her children were in the realm of physicality with a mission, and to fulfil that mission they'd need to make their own choices and find their own path through the power of their free will. If her children made poor choices, she would allow them to feel the energetic backlash of that misalignment—such a lesson was necessary. But she would never allow the backlash to be more than what was absolutely needed. If her children went astray and made decisions against her guidance, she would create an event or consequence to make them pause, reflect and reorient. But she would only ever allow her children to be utterly broken if her children needed to be completely rebuilt anew.

When her children had fallen into the pits of forgetting and had been enmeshed into the dimension of the fear-based matrix, she knew they would endure intense trauma since the Anunnaki powerfully influenced this dimension. But she knew that each traumatic experience within the fear-based matrix was an opportunity to catalyse change and a reorientation of freedom-based decision making in alignment with her guidance. So after each traumatic event endured by her children, in any dimension of the dreamscape, the Great Mother would bring her presence close and infuse her child with waves of loving support urging them to crack open their energetic armour and to feel the waves of fear that would set them free. After trauma, the Great Mother's presence would be felt strongest for all souls within the dreamscape, for it was after trauma that each soul could be catalysed into more love and remember more deeply their true nature. The Great Mother also knew that after trauma, the Anunnaki infiltration would attempt to keep those in the fear-based matrix locked into a shock induced paralysis where they would bury and suppress the fires for transformation deep within, and the soul would fall further into a pit of fear and forgetting.

What the Great Mother knew with the most certainty was that the Anunnaki was not a beast to be feared. Indeed, she could alchemize their existence into love in a split second. After all, she was the organic true nature of the dreamscape. Her children too held this same power, and she knew they simply had to realise that was the case in order to be free.

When the human beings woke up to the true nature of reality within the dreamscape and remembered the aspect of the Eternal Ocean of Light they truly were, they lived each day of their incarnation in the dimension of Heaven—connected to the organic beauty of their natural surroundings, creating with the free-flowing inspiration that moved through them. Living in the dimension of Heaven did not mean that the human beings could not see or notice the fear-based matrix or the infiltration of the Anunnaki within the dreamscape. In fact, the awakened souls could see the multidimensional nature of the dreamscape and could see fellow men and women within their neighbouring surroundings who existed geographically very close to them, but dimensionally very far away. A man living in the dimension of Heaven in one house could be neighbours with a woman in the fear-based matrix. The dimensions of the dreamscape were layered, and from the dimension of Heaven, all were visible—but from, the dimension of the fear-based matrix there was only one rigid linear reality.

Everyone in the dimension of Heaven was anchored in a state of love because they remembered the true nature of their existence and thus were in complete resonance with the organic frequency of the dreamscape in its purest form. The souls experiencing life in Heaven were in complete vibrational attunement with the Eternal Ocean of Light as well as the Great Mother and all she had created. Thus, it was easy for these men and women to speak directly to the Eternal Ocean of Light and the Great Mother. In Heaven, a direct line of conversation was accessible; a man or woman would need to simply close their eyes and feel their own loving nature so that the whispers of the Great Mother's guidance could speak through them. Since connection with her children in Heaven was of most ease, the Great Mother and the Eternal Ocean of Light spoke to these men and women the most. And these sacred souls became the messenger people who would receive downloads from Creation itself to carry forward for all souls of the dreamscape to assist their sacred missions.

In the linear time year of 2041 within the dreamscape, seven particular souls were incarnated, and they existed in the dimension of Heaven. These seven souls, including five women and two men, were scattered across the Earth geographically. The men and women lived their lives in the lead-up to 2041 experiencing parallel realities—lives orchestrated by the Great Mother that would prepare each of them individually to come together as one with a shared monumental mission—to destroy the Anunnaki presence within the dreamscape.

The team of seven within the dreamscape were being trained, by every unique life experience, to have no fear of evil. Fearlessness in the face of evil was the means by which the Anunnaki would be destroyed. True fearlessness was not cultivated by denying fear and pushing it down. It was cultivated by feeling fear. To have no fear of fear itself is to become fearless. And thus the seven human souls in this story were guided to experience and know the essence of fear in a way no other man or woman could.

Chapter Thirteen

Now the tale of the dreamscape will delve even deeper, beyond the fabric of the nature of the dreamscape realm and into the lives of seven particular human beings who incarnated together in the linear time year of 2041.

What I am about to share with you is the tale of the Sacred Seven. A tale that has never been told before. A tale that exists in the realm somewhere between fact and fiction. This tale is not a true recount of the past, since it details events from somewhere in the linear time future. And yet, this tale is indeed based on fact, since the very fabric of it pulls at the essence of truth within the heart, within your sacred heart.

The Sacred Seven were simple, ordinary men and women who existed within the dreamscape. They weren't superhero characters, nor did they possess any particular skills or traits that separated them from the rest of humanity. But what they shared with one another was a mission, assigned to them at birth, to one day unite as one force of change for the betterment of all of humanity.

Let's begin with the story of the first of the seven, Dario.

Dario was born in England. He was the son of a working-class mother and father, who knew the hardships of raising five children on a pittance. He grew up in a home wound tight by the frequency of his mother's unexpressed emotions. A palpable tension thickened the air in all corners of the home—from the narrow wallpapered staircase, to the worn down two-seater couch that pointed towards the small television set in the corner of the living room. The home was not void of love, since love lived within the heart of each person in the family. But love could find no passageway of expression through the home, since the pain of survival in the face of inner-city poverty had swallowed up the joy of free-flowing love.

Alcohol was Dario's father's elixir for coping. After a ten-hour day of driving a taxi, he would visit his second home, the local alehouse, and relax into his usual stool at the end of the bar where he would drink a steady flow of three pints between the hours of 6 p.m. and 8 p.m. When he'd arrive home, Dario's mother, exhausted and frustrated, would reject his advances. "There's your dinner," she'd mutter as she pointed to the cold meal that had been waiting on the dining table. Dario's father longed for intimacy with his wife, but the pub had a grip on him that clouded his judgement. Dario's mother longed to be chosen by her husband, and she waited day after day for him to make that choice. But each day she slipped deeper into the cage of abandonment and sorrow, where her hopes were shattered.

It was not a loveless home. But love had no true expression and thus the home felt loveless.

Growing up, Dario was sensitive to the energy of his home. As a teenager, he never contemplated why, but he avoided his home for as many hours as he could. As the years went by, Dario's father's dependency on alcohol only grew, and with that so did his sudden, unpredictable violent outbursts. Dario, as the eldest son, was usually the first in the firing line. As a small child, Dario's father would smack him or hit him with a belt for discipline, but as a teenager, his father clenched his open palm into a fist. Arguments would quickly escalate into full-scale beatings, and by age seventeen, Dario decided with certainty to get as far away from his home and his city as possible.

With no money behind him and a fire of unexpressed rage ablaze within, Dario joined the British army, and they deployed him to Afghanistan to serve as a private before long.

It was a choice that felt like freedom to a teenager imprisoned by the bars of a chaotic family home, but Dario had unknowingly signed up to experience unthinkable trauma.

Each day on the field of duty in Afghanistan, Dario would witness and experience horrors and atrocities not meant for the tenderness of the human heart. Day after day, he would walk alongside his fellow British soldiers with an M16 rifle in his hands, feeling the weight of his uniform restricting his breath as the harshness of the dry sun scorched down on his pale English cheeks. His whole body would pulse with the pounding beat of his heart, his back running with sweat beneath the layers of fabric covering him. His head would dart from left to right as he crept across the sandy expanses—waiting, watching, anticipating the sound of a violent pop that could end anyone's life, including his, at any moment.

In Afghanistan, Dario learnt to live suspended in a state of continual fear. Even as he slept, all the muscles in his body would be taut in anticipation of a deadly wake-up call. Every day he would jerk awake with the startling sound of a horn. He slept in fear; he awoke in fear; he served his duty in fear. His commanders called it "courage"—the courage to fight for Britain and to fight against evil and injustice. Some nights, Dario's body would tremble uncontrollably as he tried to sleep, and when he fell asleep, he'd dream of bloody murder and awake with his sheets soaked in sweat.

Dario stayed in Afghanistan for three full years. His time in military duty changed him to the core. The fear that had once startled him into terror had transformed into what felt like the essence of his nature. He had witnessed his closest comrades murdered before his eyes, and equally he had pulled the trigger himself as a perpetrator of violence against the innocence of strangers.

He arrived home in England, not shaken, but numb. He didn't feel angry, nor sad; in fact, he felt nothing. But it was the feeling of nothingness that became the source of a whole new paradigm of self-perpetuating problems. Dario ached to feel. He ached to love, to cry and to laugh, but he had forgotten how to access such primal forms of expression. In his desperation to feel, he clung to any experience that triggered within him some form of response, physical or emotional. The feeling of sex with a stranger brought him back into his visceral senses and anchored him in his feeling body for just long enough for the agony of his chaotic thoughts to subside. He chased sex with strangers as a temporary antidote for his relentless suffering. Like a band-aid that alleviated his hurts but did not stick, he always needed to find another. Cocaine, MDMA, crack and even heroin—he found a distorted form of love for these chemical compounds and the euphoric highs that would temporarily burst through the mundane hum of perpetual nothingness.

The solace drugs and sex brought to Dario quickly developed into something far darker. His dependency on drugs magnetized dangerous criminals into his life, and before long, Dario found himself in his darkest hour.

Crouched in a ball in the corner of a dreary sixth-story council flat, he needed help. He had owed a group of renowned inner-city gangsters two thousand pounds for four months. As the sound of fists hammered on the front door of the flat, Dario, penniless and terrified, knew that the moment the men broke in, there would be no mercy.

The men continued to thump on the door, and Dario had no choice but to uncurl himself from the cowering ball and stand up to assess his options for his escape. If he didn't, he knew he would be a dead man. The open window close to him caught his attention, and unlike most

English flats, this window opened wide enough for a possible—although potentially fatal—escape. Dario, without thought, climbed his thin and malnourished body slowly out to sit perched on the edge of the ledge, wrapping his arm back inside the window to hold on tight to the adjoining wall within. He looked down at the six-story fall beneath him and knew that a free fall jump could cost his life, or at least a couple of broken limbs. He quickly glanced from side to side, but there wasn't a drainpipe or adjacent balcony within reach to offer another option. Directly beneath him was a white van that might break his fall if he was lucky enough to land directly on its roof. The banging continued, and Dario sat, suspended on the window ledge six stories up, glancing over his right shoulder at the front door, waiting to learn his fate. His heart was racing. Despite all he had been through in Afghanistan, this was the first moment in his life that he truly believed it could be the end. Dario could hear that the door thumping had escalated into powerful kicks aimed at bringing the door down.

That moment changed everything for Dario. He closed his eyes, and for a second in suspended time, he felt a wave of energy flood through his body. Courage surged through his heart. Not the courage the army generals had spoken about. Not the courage that is attached to duty or patriotism. He felt the courage of an eagle soar through his pulsing heart—true courage. He felt alive, and for some strange reason, he was not afraid.

A final thud of the door blinked Dario's eyes open and, in an altered state of slowed time perception, he watched as two men charged towards him. It was as though Dario was dreaming. This couldn't be real, could it? "Jump!" a soft voice whispered to him from within the echoes of his consciousness. "Jump, Dario, and I will catch you." The men, within arm's reach, launched at Dario to rip him back from the window ledge, but just before they could, Dario pushed off from the wall with his feet and flew into the air in radical acceptance of his unknown fate.

The next thing he remembered was the sound of the heart rate monitor in the hospital ward. Was that a dream? As he blinked his eyes open, Dario knew that he'd narrowly avoided death. Some kind of miracle had saved him. The nurse arrived in his room with her clipboard in hand. "You're back!" she exclaimed. "That was quite a fall you had. How are you feeling?"

Dario didn't know how he was feeling. There were too many unknowns. Where were the men who were looking for him? Who brought him to the hospital? How long had he been out for? Feeling suddenly overwhelmed, Dario closed his eyes again and went inward. As soon as he closed his eyes, a powerful vision flooded him. Perhaps it was the painkillers? Or was he simply hallucinating? He wasn't sure, but an eagle, with the wingspan of the entire sky, filled the inner space of his consciousness, and a coherent message spoke through him. "Follow the eagle," it whispered.

Five days later, Dario was back at his mum and dad's place, staying in his old bedroom. The warmth of his mother's care and the cups of tea in bed were a welcome tonic for the coldness of the life he'd just come from. He was healing from a broken fibula, a broken collarbone and major bruising, so, lying in his old bed, staring out the window into the grey autumn clouds, he found himself bored. He couldn't go to a nightclub to pick up women, and he needed to stay as far out of sight of his old drug dealers as possible, so he began researching. He opened his old laptop and typed in the search bar: "recovering from veteran trauma". He also searched "healing PTSD". Pages of search results appeared, and not understanding what he was actually looking for, Dario clicked randomly on one link. The page opened and Dario froze, his eyes glued to the image of the bald eagle at the focal centre of the webpage. He scrolled through the page, and the picture of the eagle appeared multiple times positioned within the text of the page. Dario read the contents of the webpage that detailed an Ayahuasca healing retreat in the jungle of Peru. He had never heard of Ayahuasca, but the eagle image had sparked his curiosity. He took himself down a rabbit hole of research, learning about the healing properties of the mystical Amazonian plant blend as he lay in his bed.

After a few days of extensive research, Dario knew he needed to get to Peru. He told no one about the eagle message. He didn't want to sound insane. But within his heart, he knew something had saved him from death as he sat on that window ledge, and he was ready to follow the same inner voice to see where it would take him. And so, Dario borrowed the money from his brother with the promise of repayment, arranged his transport and set off on an adventure that would take him into the depths of the Amazon where he would unknowingly meet the inner demons that would set him free.

After six weeks in the jungle of Iquitos, Peru, and fifteen Ayahuasca ceremonies, Dario was ready to conclude his experience with his final, sixteenth ceremony. Dario had been transformed by his six weeks in the jungle. He hadn't known what to expect starting the experience, but as the retreat drew to its close, he was certain the eagle had guided him to his place of healing. His eyes were no longer clouded with yellowed whites and red veins. Instead, his eyes sparkled with aliveness, the brown of his irises etched with the same organic beauty as the bark of the trees within the jungle. His skin had healed—a dewy smooth quality had replaced the motley damaged patches. He was smiling often, not for any reason or at anything, but he was smiling often simply because he felt joy. It hadn't been easy for Dario. Each ceremony had taken him to the depths of his subconscious mind where he met the very terror he'd inflicted on those whose lives he had taken in the war. Some ceremonies forced him to feel the shame of the self-destructive patterns of harm and the damage inflicted through drug abuse. He vomited, purged and let go—deeply. During one particularly challenging ceremony, Dario met his dad and realised his dad's suppressed rage had passed onto him, which he then channelled into war and murder, passing it onto others. In that ceremony, Dario saw the entity that was masculine rage, and he felt where he had been both the victim and the perpetrator of such rage. And as he saw the entity, and felt the entity, he set it free.

As Dario walked from his hut along the jungle path towards the temple for his last ceremony, he felt a sense of deep inner pride. He had healed not just himself, but he was doing such deep inner work he was moving energetic mountains for his family and humanity. He smiled with the inner warmth of his journey as he reflected. But then, a wave of fear flooded through his body. "What am I going to do after this?" he wondered. And almost instantly, an inner voice of calm spoke through him, the same inner voice that guided him to jump from the window. "Follow the eagle," it whispered. Dario smiled in acknowledgement of his own inner guidance and continued to walk onwards towards the temple.

Dario entered the ceremony space and sat on his mat, taking his usual place within the circle awaiting the other participants.

As he sat in his usual daze of pre-ceremony anticipation, an unfamiliar woman arrived at the temple entrance. She was holding a guitar under her arm, a flute in one hand and a few strange percussion instruments in the other. She peered into the space through the opening archway, and the warmth of her smile and presence sent a wave of comfort through the entire space. The regular facilitator jumped up and headed over to greet the slight blonde woman. He introduced her as Anna. "Hey guys, to make this last ceremony extra special, Anna is going to be weaving her medicine songs into the space. We are so blessed to have her here. So please welcome Anna!"

"Hey, Anna!" a few gently chorused.

As Anna took her spot at the front of the ceremony space and arranged her instruments strategically around her mat, Dario couldn't believe what he saw—Anna's t-shirt had an image of a majestic bald eagle with its wings outstretched printed across the chest. Who was this woman? Dario didn't know what the significance of Anna's presence meant, but he knew she was of radical importance in his life.

Chapter Fourteen

I would like to take this moment to interrupt the story of the Sacred Seven within the dreamscape to share something with you that feels important.

When I was a child, I knew who I was. I remember being just six and performing dance concerts on the grass at family barbeques in England, where I would instruct distant relatives to sit quietly on their fold-out chairs whilst I danced. I would twirl and sway with my eyes closed, feeling the ecstasy of sharing my dance with those who loved me most. I would open my eyes to see the overjoyed smiles of my family beaming at me in utter delight, and I would allow the feeling of their silent praise to deepen my dance. I knew what it was to love life. I knew what it was to be absolutely free—of judgement and of fear.

My childhood was filled with opportunities to express my limitless creative capacity as a human being. I was free to dance when I wanted to. I was free to cook, sing, paint, read, draw and write. I was free to be inward; I was free to be outward.

But something at some point shattered that sense of freedom within me and replaced it with the invisible bars of fear and judgment that stopped me from dancing, singing, painting, writing and drawing. A catastrophic lie wove into my psyche that trained me to believe that life just wasn't that simple.

As I sit here writing this now, at age thirty-four, my gaze over the top of my laptop takes in an expansive hardwood jarrah window framed by an old wisteria vine dripping in spring lilac flowers that rain down on the grass outside with every gust of gentle wind. I can see green in the distance in all directions and my husband, Scott, down in the veggie garden, raking the soil in the raised beds, pulling out the old broccoli from last season and preparing new compost for the summer garden. I can hear the distant hum of Xavier Rudd—Scott's soundtrack for creation. And I can see Awen, our little four-year-old, with a Tupperware container of soil and, more than likely, worms, creating her own little reality of a garden wonderland. It's taken me many years, and much healing, but I see and feel clearly now that life is actually as simple as my six-year-old self knew it to be. In my free-flowing creativity as a writer, we are provided for. In Scott's overflowing passion for the garden, we are provided for.

And so the question is: If we continued our entire lives in a childlike wonder where all we did was create freely and limitlessly whilst following the impulses of our hearts, would everything work out okay? From my humble perspective as I share this with you now, I feel the answer to that question is yes—better than okay—we would live the lives we were always intended to live—inspired, happy, limitless, free.

When I shared my performances at family barbeques as a child, I do not remember ever contemplating if people would like my dance. I never considered for a moment if my dance was good or bad. There was no inner space for concern around whether I was taking up too much space or if I was too much. All I remember was the innocence of my sharing and how true it felt to me to offer the gift of my expression to my family. But above all, I remember the faces of joy that were reflecting back to me when I danced. I remember the frequency of delight that my pure expression brought to those moments in time for all involved.

And now as I write this to share with you, I do so for joy. I do so because I want to. I don't know if this story will ever be published, or if it will reach all corners of the world. Because I now realise creation is not about an outcome, it is about an impulse to birth something into being that has never been before.

When I danced as a child, the impulse to create a moment of beauty moved through me, and I allowed it to be expressed. But what was it that birthed the inner impulse into being? Perhaps it was something so multifaceted that I could have never understood it as a child. Perhaps a distant aunty was struggling and needed an injection of pure joy into her day? Perhaps the song I chose to sing reminded my mum of what a good job she was doing in a moment of defeat? And why is it I am called to share this particular story? I have no idea, but I am writing it, and thus I trust that even one particular soul will read these words and will be reminded spontaneously of their pure creative innocence that the world needs so deeply right now.

To heal is to alchemize our fear of creating freely.

To create freely is to live in Heaven on Earth.

Chapter Fifteen

Now back to the story of the Sacred Seven. The second of the seven was a woman named Anna.

It was evident from a very young age Anna had a gift. Anna grew up in a musical household. Her father had made a name for himself as a folk musician, and her mother had received classical training as a singer. Anna never knew what it was to learn music, just as most people never remember the moments of learning to walk or talk. To Anna, music just was. And rhythm was as innate to her as any of her primal instincts.

As a teenager, Anna was selected as a member of a prestigious classical choir. A privilege bestowed only upon the most talented voices. She practiced and performed religiously. Her vocal coach critiqued her song, and then she perfected it to the degree of a precise science, more so than an art form. It didn't take long for young Anna to fall out of love with the choir. Her commitment to the choir felt like a form of torture to her creative purity, and she felt she had no choice but to cut ties to her teachers, the choir and all aspects of performative singing.

The Eternal Ocean of Light and the Great Mother had a plan for Anna, as they did for all their children. But as a soul, Anna had incarnated with a specific mission, and the gift of her voice was a key to her fulfilling that mission. Unlocking the true limitless power of her voice as a healing tool was Anna's destiny, and she was being guided by a ferociously loving power to realise that destiny above all else.

From an early age, Anna felt connected to a higher power. She believed deeply in signs and synchronicities, and because of her belief, the Great Mother moved freely through her, illuminating her path with absolute clarity. After leaving the choir, Anna found a community Kirtan where Bhakti Yogis would come together at the town hall every Friday night to sing, free from inhibitions, from the heart. Men, women and children of all ages would gather at the musty-smelling old community centre and transform a lifeless government building into a temple of candlelit devotion through song. The bellow of the reverberant harmonium played by the Kirtan leaders would vibrate into the chambers of her heart, and as she sang along, without refinement or scrutiny, her own song would vibrate into the same inner space and transport her into a realm of pure love.

Every week Anna would attend Kirtan, and before long, she too assisted in leading others through the devotional journey of sung collective prayer. Every time she attended Kirtan, she felt as though a direct line of connection to God opened through the channel of her song. To her, it was as though the vibration of her own sound was in complete resonance with the primordial sound of existence. Her "Om" was a wave that she could surf all the way home to God, and the more she recognised that power within her sound, the more love would flood through her body.

The Great Mother knew her regular Kirtan practice was transporting Anna directly into the dimension of Heaven, where a clear line of audible connection would be activated and where Anna would receive specific guidance from the Great Mother for the absolute fulfilment of her divine mission and destiny.

Before long, Anna had forgotten what it was to sing for the validation of others. Her song was no longer a precise science but a vibration tool for connection. She had mastered her sound, not to be audibly pleasing but to attune to different dimensional frequencies and transform those frequencies. Anna explored channelling her song into healing experiences for groups and developed a psychic sense that allowed her to see energy. Through her devotional practice, she'd mastered the skill of seeing and sensing the energy of a room and all those within it. She could see distortions and fractures of fear beyond the visible light spectrum, and she could attune her voice to meet the fear and then transform it into the pure harmonic resonance of love.

Anna had explored working with crystal singing bowls and crystal harps, but she found nothing could transform energy as potently as the power of her own voice. And thus, living in a world full of distortion, Anna hummed down supermarket aisles and toned under her breath in the queue at the post office. She was sensitive to energy with the ability to transform it, and simultaneously, she existed in a world where she could see and feel fear all around her.

One day, Aisha, a good friend of Anna's from Kirtan, asked her if she wanted to meet The Mother with her. Anna did not know what Aisha meant by this, but she was curious. Aisha told Anna about the spirit of the Great Mother that lived within a plant medicine called Ayahuasca. Anna was afraid. She'd heard horror stories about people meeting demons, being taken into the pits of fiery hell and vomiting for hours on end with this plant medicine.

"What if I go into this realm and never come back? What if I shit myself?" Anna asked with curiosity as she expressed her fears.

Aisha giggled. "There is a Great Mother," she went on to reply, "who is the mother of all people, the Earth, the sky and the cosmos, and she loves you more than life itself. Wouldn't you be curious to know if that love has a message for you?" Anna gulped. She knew when her heart was pulling her towards an experience that she was intended to have, even when she was terrified of it.

With an enormous sigh of anticipation, she agreed. "Okay. I feel it's calling me," said Anna. She confirmed her space for the ceremony, gave $300 to Aisha and began mentally preparing for the weekend ahead.

Aisha had told her to set an intention and that The Mother would respond to that intention. So after some contemplation, Anna wrote her clear intention on the front page of her brand new journal.

Great Mother, I am ready to remember the true power of my gifts. Show me who I truly am. Show me why I am here on this Earth at this time. Free me from all fears so I can fulfil my mission, whatever that may be. – Anna

Just a few days later, Anna was telepathically speaking her intention into the cup of thick brown medicine she anxiously held in her hands. The sun had set, and in the candlelit teepee of a dusk full moon, she was the last of twelve to be called to the altar to drink. She'd driven over an hour to the fifty-acre property on the outskirts of the city, but as she sat in the dark tent nervously anticipating what the Great Mother had in store for her, she felt as though she was a million miles from the comfort of her bed.

With a final shaky exhale, she put the cup to her lips and gulped it down. She'd never experienced a taste like it. The viscous bitterness of the liquid lingered on the inside of her mouth. She resisted the urge to dry retch out of respect for the shaman, who had flown from Brazil to serve the medicine, and handed the cup back to him, bowing her head in a prayer of gratitude. Anna returned to her mat and sat in silent meditation, waiting patiently to feel the effects of the medicine.

After a long pause of collective silence, the rhythmic sound of a rattle echoed through the space and with it, a tuneful whistle. It was as though the medicine and the sounds were interconnected, and the shaman was whistling to the liquid within each person's body, activating a dormant frequency of magic. Anna felt an intense wave of energy flood up through her body—from her toes, slowly rolling up into her spine, opening her heart and her throat—and she let out an uncontrollable sigh. The energy was overwhelming, but she knew she just needed to breathe. With a deep and intentional breath, Anna allowed the intensity of the energy to continue moving through her. She wasn't simply observing the intensity; she was the intensity. The energy was opening her whole body from the inside out; an interdimensional tidal wave of pleasure surged up through every cell of her body. Her mind and awareness dissolved, and when the intensity met her internal headspace, a kaleidoscopic explosion of crystalline whites and purples merged her fully into a realm of oneness.

She was home. Time dissolved. All sense of Anna dissolved, and she became merged with the infinite space of nothingness. It was a realm of pure peace and infinite possibility—like an ocean of light with no beginning and no end. She was not simply observing this realm; she was the ocean of light. Perhaps she existed in this realm for just a moment, or perhaps it was for hours, but a surge of creative excitement flushed through her body that switched her in an instant from infinite peace and light to a dreamscape of creativity and wonder. The dreamscape revealed itself to her, along with the true nature of reality and all the souls who exist within it. Anna saw clearly how the Eternal Ocean of Light consciously dreamed the dreamscape into being, and how the Great Mother was the energy of pure creation within the Earth realm.

Anna was in awe and amazement. Her conscious awareness had returned, and she was in witness of the most spectacular visual showcase revealing the true nature of reality. What an honour, she reflected as she lay smiling in wonder.

Her vision suddenly turned dark. Everything changed. Her heart pulsed as though it would jump from her chest, and fear flushed through her body. The voice of The Mother spoke to her: "If creation births life into perfection, destruction decays life into chaos." The essence of her words felt nauseating within Anna's body. Everything The Mother had shown her so far felt like absolute pure truth, but this felt untrue—distorted.

A portal of vision opened from the darkness and Anna saw anti-life matter dripping from the fabric of creation. The vision made no logical sense to her, but she felt it as a message. Anti-life energy was like the pus that drains from an abscess. She saw this anti-life matter oozing from the realm of the dreamscape into a black hole—an abyss of lifelessness. The anti-life matter had consciousness, but the consciousness was of destruction. This consciousness could not birth anything into being since to birth is to give life, but, the anti-life consciousness could multiply into more anti-life matter—just as cancer cells can multiply. Through this process, the anti-life consciousness multiplied into a realm of chaos, disorder and evil. The realm reeked of death and decay. The beings who inhabited the realm stunk of death and cast no beauty. All beings and things in the anti-life realm were hideous and becoming more hideous in each moment, since that was the nature of the anti-life fabric of reality.

Anna felt the putrid essence of this anti-life realm and, with that, a sudden wave of nausea pulled her stomach into a knot of agony. She lost her conscious awareness once more and her whole body and consciousness was plunged into the realm of anti-life matter. Anna groaned and moaned as the putrid stench of death and evil swallowed her up. She was pulled into the depths of hell: a realm of black sticky tar pulsing with the nauseating frequency of fear. All around her she saw hideous beings snarling at her. Their eyes like deep tunnels of black with not a speck of light to be found. She fell deeper and deeper into the anti-life realm until she landed at the centre of it. She knew it was the centre, because she saw a black-cloaked figure of absolute power and evil with a face hidden by a shadow. Fear pulsed through her body to such a degree she felt as though she would die. Was this the root of all evil, she wondered? Her vision took her closer to the figure where she could feel the immense power of evil that lived behind the cloaked figure. The black-cloaked figure took its skeletal hand up to its hood as though it was about to reveal the true nature of its hidden face. But before the reveal, Anna was shunted out of the vision and returned to the reality of the teepee.

She opened her eyes and, breathless, she tried to calm herself back into the comfort of her mat and the space. She tried to remind herself it was just an Ayahuasca journey, and that she was safe, but she was shaken and afraid. Her body lay on the mat trembling with fear as she stared at the apex of the teepee above in shock.

For a while, Anna lay on her mat, trying to calm her breath slowly in disbelief of where the medicine had taken her. That was so intense, she reflected. She couldn't believe what she saw and how real it all seemed. Slightly traumatised, a wave of energy returned to her body, like a massage of pure love, weaving through any layers of fear or trauma from her experience. She suddenly felt like a toddler, being nurtured by the warm embrace of the most tender mother in all of existence. And as this love intensified, Anna sobbed. She let out waves of tears and released all tension stored in her body—not just from the intense journey but from her entire life.

As she sobbed into the embrace of pure unconditional love, The Mother spoke to her again. This time with an unshakable certainty that Anna could not ignore: "Anna, you just met the root of all evil—the Anunnaki. You are not ready yet, but soon you will be. The Earth is a birthing place, and you, my child, are here to rebirth the Earth and all her children." Fireworks of light and kaleidoscopic fractals of perfection exploded in Anna's vision and she spent the rest of the journey in pure ecstasy and wonder.

Chapter Sixteen

Now that you have been introduced to both Dario and Anna, let's continue to delve even deeper into the tale of the Sacred Seven within the dreamscape.

When the Eternal Ocean of Light consciously birthed a dreamscape and individualised souls into being, this birthing process was an expression of love. The creative birthing energy of the Great Mother was, in its essence, pure love. Everything the Eternal Ocean of Light dreamed into being expressed perfection since the Eternal Ocean of Light could only create perfectly.

The Eternal Ocean of Light was aware of malignant anti-life energies that had multiplied into a realm of chaos and was aware that this realm of chaos had manifested into individualised beings of evil—collectively named the Anunnaki. Infesting the dreamscape realm, the Anunnaki were attempting to cast all of life into chaos and destruction, while the Eternal Ocean of Light and the Great Mother watched on. The wise and infinite creators of the dreamscape knew that the infiltration of anti-life Anunnaki would assist the souls of the dreamscape in their sacred mission of remembering their infinite true nature, but only up to a certain point. There was indeed a point of no return where the Anunnaki presence within the dreamscape was ultimately harmful to the greater mission. There was an energetic tipping point where the Anunnaki presence within the dreamscape would no longer be catalytic for soul awakening, but would be like a poison of anti-life chaos that would consume the dreamscape into its own anti-life realm of hell.

Two momentous forces were accelerating rapidly: that of humanity's collective awakening, and that of the Anunnaki's nefarious plan for domination. These two colliding forces were intertwined, catalysing one another into more momentum. The Anunnaki plan thrust humanity into a rapid awakening. And humanity's awakening darkened the Anunnaki plan. Based on the speed of these two interwoven forces, a tipping point in the dreamscape's linear time perception became apparent to the Great Mother and the Eternal Ocean of Light. In the linear time year of 2041, one force would win—love or fear—with either force exterminating the other.

The Great Mother needed to orchestrate the awakening of her children so perfectly that the Anunnaki would serve constructively until the moment of the energetic tipping point of no return—when the Anunnaki would need to be destroyed. Not a moment before, not a moment after. This was easy for the Great Mother since she only orchestrated the dreamscape perfectly. Even so, her children were guiding their individualised lives according to their own free will, and thus there was an unknown element for the Great Mother and the Eternal Ocean of Light. Would their children obey and heed the obvious signs presented to them and rise to remember who they are before the energetic tipping point of no return? Would the men and women of the dreamscape recognise their unconscious fears and traumas and use these as catalytic embers to activate their fire of limitless creative potential?

Humanity's free will was the only variable that could sway the fate of the dreamscape in either direction—that of a unified utopia for all to live connected with the true essence of creation, or that of a manifest dimension of decaying hell, void of love.

The Great Mother continued to weave signs and synchronicities into the dreamscape to wake her children up from the fear-based matrix and to assist in their ascension into the dimension of Heaven. She knew her role in humanity's mission, and she was unwavering in her loving commitment to assisting her children. But as the energetic tipping point drew closer, the Eternal Ocean of Light knew a further intervention would be necessary to assist all beings within the dreamscape to fulfil their assigned mission. Of course, the Eternal Ocean of Light could, with a flash, end the dreamscape and return all of creation back to the frequency of oneness. But that would make the entire dreamscape experiment redundant, pointless, and the Eternal Ocean of Light was not ready for such an abrupt conclusion to the marvel of creation without witnessing the souls he'd dreamed into being organically reclaim their truth.

And so the Eternal Ocean of Light dreamed up a means of subtle intervention that could have a powerful impact in guiding the free will of all men and women towards their sacred remembering. The Great Mother had been busy, speaking to and guiding all her children ceaselessly. But what if there were more sources of guidance to illuminate the highest path for human beings, the Eternal Ocean of Light pondered? What if there were a myriad of higher consciousness voices of guidance that could assist the men and women of the dreamscape to crystallise their divinely guided free will? Who would these beings be? And what would be the nature of their existence? The Eternal Ocean of Light considered, for these beings to offer telepathically delivered guidance of the purest loving nature, these beings would need to be of pure consciousness themselves. These beings would already need to know themselves as aspects of oneness and would need to exist for the sole purpose of humanity's assistance—individualised consciousness attuned to the frequency of eternal service, beyond limits.

As the Eternal Ocean of Light pondered, the dreamed idea of such an individualised being of higher consciousness manifested instantly into a crystalline plasma being in humanoid shape. This being was translucent, not dense in physical matter like the human body, and yet individualised and separate from the source of its creator. Since the plasma being was completely one with the consciousness of the Eternal Ocean of Light, it could create its own reality and realm. The plasma being spoke using pure sound frequency, instead of comprehensible language. Through pure sound frequency expressed, he told the Eternal Ocean of Light that he was called Andromeda.

Andromeda held a similar frequency to the human beings who lived within the dimension of Heaven within the dreamscape. Although, since Andromeda did not need to navigate a realm of physicality, his consciousness was more clear and expansive. Andromeda didn't have a creative life-force energy moving through his body inspiring him to work and birth new visions like human souls—he was content in pure beingness, though he was motivated by his innate purpose, which was to serve and guide humanity. A home realm such as a dreamscape wasn't necessary for Andromeda, since he was already fully realised as an aspect of the Eternal Ocean of Light. But the light-being knew that if he were surrounded by other beings of the same frequency as his, he could magnify his power and guidance for human beings. And so Andromeda manifested into form one hundred more plasma light-beings, nearly identical to himself but with varying individualised expressions of the same consciousness.

As 101 unified Andromedans, the plasma beings took the hands of one another. In a circle of pure consciousness and divine intent, they manifested a realm for themselves to rest within and to plan sacred woven intentions to influence the free will of humanity in alignment with the organically assigned mission. As individualised consciousnesses, each Andromedan being had the power to merge fully with individual human souls in particular moments of their lives. Part of the Andromedan plan for dreamscape intervention was to merge with a human being in certain times of darkness, and thus to raise the frequency of the person to loving oneness in that moment. The Andromedans knew the power of the frequency of loving oneness in destroying the Anunnaki, since loving oneness actually alchemized fear into love. The more of humanity that was anchored in loving oneness, the more absolute would be the destruction of the Anunnaki.

A healer by the name of Jerry was doing powerful work within the dreamscape. Jerry was in close communion with the Great Mother and the Eternal Ocean of Light, and although he'd had a life that once took him into the depths of the fear-based matrix, he had found his way out and was committed to following his creative truth as a teacher and leader of the healing arts within the dimension of Heaven.

Jerry travelled the world offering group healing sessions to anyone who needed it. He travelled Asia, Europe and the USA offering a unique blend of Qigong infused with his own intuitively guided energetic practice. Miracles would take place in Jerry's sessions. Children with behavioural issues would suddenly calm, and the elderly with joint pain would suddenly find relief. The tangible results he continued to see motivated him. Although, he was tired. He worked hard and travelled continually, and he felt at times that his mission asked a great deal from him.

In the linear time year of 2026 within the dreamscape, Jerry was facilitating a group healing session for seventy souls in Dubai. The morning before the session, Jerry felt exhausted. He was at breaking point, and he didn't know how he was going to manage the day ahead. The seventy people who had booked tickets had huge expectations for their own miracles and were projecting those expectations energetically towards Jerry. This was usually the case for his sessions but, on this particular morning in Dubai, for the first time, Jerry felt the magnitude of the invisible weight of the responsibility he was carrying. And so, in the cramped corner of his twelfth-story hotel room, Jerry knelt down and brought his hands into a devotional mudra of prayer. He needed help, and he wasn't shy about asking. He knew a divinely orchestrated force had brought him to this point in his life and that the same force would show up to help him in his time of exhaustion. Jerry spoke his prayer out loud.

Mother, Father—God, thank you so much for all the blessings you have brought to me. Thank you for this sacred opportunity to serve from my heart. Thank you for my life of alignment, inspiration, freedom and creativity. Please help me today. Please charge me with life-force energy and vitality. Please assist me in serving every single person in attendance today to my fullest capacity. I give myself to your divine grace and wisdom. Please work through me. And so it is.

Jerry trusted, with the fullness of his heart, the power of his prayer. He knew the entire day was taken care of by a higher order, and he felt his divine connection amplified from his moment of prayer.

Later that day, after the lunch break, in the second portion of the healing workshop, Jerry gathered the seventy participants to sit in a circle on the floor. The energy was high. Many of the participants had already had profound experiences of kundalini activation, trauma release and psychic downloads. A bubble of excitable chatter fluttered around the circle as the group waited in anticipation to be guided through the next portion of the day.

Jerry was never exactly sure how he would lead each session, but his commitment was to serve as an open channel of love where higher wisdom would guide him, moment by moment. In preparation to begin the session, Jerry took his place sitting alongside the participants in the circle. He closed his eyes and took a few steady, intentional breaths to anchor his awareness into his infinite heart. A voice whispered to him from the echo chambers of his heart.

"Jerry, we are with you," it said.

Jerry slowly blinked his eyes open; a blue hue tinted the entire room. An aquamarine mist floated mystically through the centre of the circle. He glanced at each participant; their eyes were closed and their bodies limp and floppy, although sat upright. It was as though the blue mist had sedated each person into an altered state—a hypnotic trance with no conscious awareness. Jerry was consciously aware and present, seemingly unaffected by the blue mist, but he felt awash with calm. His limbs became heavy, and his physical body dense, as though it didn't want to move. He became suspended in absolute stillness, and his visual perception of the surrounding space crystallised to allow him to see the subtle coding and geometry of the fabric of reality. Within the blue fog, Jerry could see the crystalline double helices of each person's DNA spiralling through and around their bodies. He could see that some helices had damage or fractures while others were augmented from their organic nature. Jerry's vision guided him to one particular woman. Her DNA appeared flawless. A smooth dance of the crystalline double helix rotated up her spine, opening her to a cosmos of geometric perfection—a universal star system that was her own harmonic auric field. The woman's harmonic aura expanded from her field in fractal diamond coding and appeared to enter the energetic fields of each of the other participants, repairing their damaged and augmented DNA strands back into their organic crystalline perfection.

Jerry, in his own suspended state of trance and wonder, watched on, his whole body vibrating with the crystalline energy of the room. He looked down at his heart and saw that he too was emanating his own diamond coding of harmonic perfection around the circle. He and the woman were unconsciously performing a mass healing of absolute DNA repair, simply from their own state of beingness—their own organic, healed essence.

Suddenly the room began vibrating more intensely. A deafening hum, like the buzz of a thousand bees, sounded through the circle. Each participant's body was shaking, trembling to the vibrational hum that reverberated through the space. What was happening? Jerry wondered in amazement as he surrendered to the shaking of his own body, his eyelids growing heavier. The energy intensified, and the blue fog transformed into a sapphire and diamond grid formation of clear crystal lines that orchestrated the circle into a tightly woven geometrical vortex of healing energy. The vibration intensified further, and Jerry's conscious awareness flickered from observational amazement to absolute dissolution of self—and back and forth he flickered. Through the haze of his heavy eyelids, Jerry saw there was a circle of beings that surrounded them. A circle of several avatar blue plasma beings stood in silent presence, hand to hand, casting Jerry and the group into a vortex of crystalline energy. Who were these beings, Jerry wondered? Before he found the answer, he fell into a deep sleep.

When Jerry awoke, spellbound and disoriented, he peered around the room through sleepy eyes and saw each participant well and smiling, as though they were each awakening from a deep and profoundly insightful meditation. Whispered chatter of excited bewilderment spread through the room, and Jerry caught the eye of the woman he'd witnessed in perfect energetic resonance unconsciously performing the mass healing with him and the blue plasma beings. The woman slowly walked over to Jerry and stood directly in front of him, tenderly holding his eye contact as both welled up with watery tears of loving admiration for one another. The woman slowly reached out and placed her hand on the centre of Jerry's chest. She closed her eyes as though all that existed in that moment was the pulse of Jerry's love that she needed to honour silently through her loving touch. Jerry too closed his eyes to receive the sacred moment of tenderness and connection. After a few moments, they blinked their eyes open and their joyful smiles deepened into a childlike giggle. They did not know what was happening, but they knew that magic was real, life was extraordinary and that an unexplainably spectacular source of support connected them.

For months after the Dubai event, Jerry received correspondence from the seventy participants giving him feedback and detailing the unexplainable transformation that had taken place in their lives since the healing. Many of the participants were healers themselves, and several of them were recounting stories of their gifts becoming amplified and the presence of light-beings appearing in their dreams and their visions. Jerry was receiving feedback of spontaneous cancer remission, miraculous manifestation of aligned opportunities and sudden alleviation of ailments like anxiety and depression.

The most profound email Jerry received after the event was from Jane, the woman he'd shared the sacred moment of connection with in Dubai. Jane explained to Jerry that she was a psychic astrologer and that she'd been in contact with a group of high-dimensional light-beings known as the Andromedans. They had spoken through her with a message for him, and she had written the message for Jerry in the email.

Jerry,

Well done. You have trained well for this moment, and now your actual work begins. A moment will come when you will be called upon. You will be called to a stadium for mass healing. We will be there to support you, as well as many others. In the year 2041, everything will be decided, and humanity's fate will be revealed. Keep going. Keep practicing. We will call upon you—and Jane as well.

As Jerry read Jane's email, goose bumps rippled across his skin, and he felt an electric tingle surge from the crown of his head down his spine. He felt the truth in the words, and spontaneous tears spilled down his cheeks. From the inner realms of his heart, he sobbed. He cried with the honour it was to be chosen for such a mission and the gratitude for the magic of service and healing in his life. How far he had come from his old life. How ready he was to serve others to the fullness of his capacity. From that moment on, the words in Jane's email ignited a fire for service in Jerry's heart that would not be extinguished. His fatigue was gone. His mission intensified. And his commitment to nurturing his connection to the beings of light who assisted him and anointed him with his sacred mission became the focal point of every moment of his day.

With each year that went by, Jerry's connection deepened. His powers grew. And he waited patiently for his moment to be called upon.

Chapter Seventeen

I'd like to continue sharing with you the tale of the Sacred Seven within the dreamscape.

Before Jane's serendipitous meeting with Jerry, she was being guided along her own divinely orchestrated path of waking up to the true nature of reality, beyond the veils of fear and distortion.

Jane was an academic. She had a sharp mind and an acute eye for detail. For the first few decades of her life, Jane lived within a fear-based matrix of her own making. Her logical mind and her perpetual need to analyse and find evidence to explain every detail had pushed her into a linear dimensional prison of limited possibility. Her sacred, infinite nature drew her to obsess over the stars in the night sky. The stars were integral to her divine mission. However, from the fear-based matrix ruled by her conditioned logical mind, the only possible way she could conceive of exploring the stars was through scientific study. Jane became an astronomer and pursued her academic field as far as it could take her.

It was in the final years of her study for her PhD in astronomy that cracks within the veil of Jane's perception formed. The Great Mother stood by as these sacred cracks opened for Jane to see the truth of the dreamscape and indeed of herself as a soul existing within it. The Great Mother wove her magic into Jane's days, speaking to her through numerology and equations—the language that Jane's soul resonated with most. And the Great Mother cast into Jane's field, through an internet advertisement, an online training in Vedic astrology.

Everything about the online training would usually have Jane cringing. The "qualified in ten weeks" nature of the program was laughable to a doctor of astronomy in the making. And she'd always referred to astrology as a quackery of spiritual nonsense for the desperate—completely without evidence and unprovable. Despite all of her usual judgments, something about this online training had caught her attention. Perhaps it was the branding, or the colours of the webpage. Perhaps it was the marketing copy and the sales strategies on the landing page. But actually, it was the synchronistic timing of a training of monumental significance arriving into her awareness on the day where the crack in her perception had completely shattered the false paradigm she lived within the day before.

Jane purchased the training and began her fastidious study of Vedic astrology. She became consumed with the content. As she read every page of the manual, it was as though she already knew the information and was rereading something she'd previously written herself. She ran out of time to complete the thesis that was due for her PhD, and so she paused her studies, absolutely enamoured with the online training, consumed by a science that felt ancient to her soul. Jane didn't just read the content; she devoured it. She soaked up the essence of the true meaning of the stars, and with each concept that landed within the fabric of her cells, another veil of her distorted linear perception would lift.

Jane's impeccable mind and logical thinking suddenly collided with something infinitely powerful—the truth. And suddenly, the years of study as an astronomer felt redundant and of no intrinsic value. Her common sense dismantled the complex falsities of stars she had learned. That's when Jane became completely bewildered, lost and without purpose. She reflected on how many years she'd dedicated to concepts that no longer seemed relevant. She fell into a depression—into a void of worthlessness, where her life had no meaning. She had defined herself as an academic, and since her study now felt wasted, she became consumed by the heaviness of a redundant life. It was a weight of suffering she felt ashamed to share—since she had no community around her that could see life through the same veil of perception she now did. She was alone. And so, from that loneliness, she had nowhere to turn but within.

Jane, hopeless and in pain, turned herself inwards—away from the stars—into the depths of her heart and her body, where she met her limitless true nature as an aspect of the Eternal Ocean of Light. She became committed to her inward journey of healing and meditation. Unsure what the path ahead held, she focused every fragment of her awareness into the eternal present moment and realised quickly that every piece of information she had ever searched for or studied towards lived within her.

With that realisation, Jane would sit for hours in silent meditation, directing her internal focus into the infinite space within her heart. Within the blackness of the infinite cavern within her chest, she could see the stars, the moon and all of creation. In a peaceful trance, Jane could pierce through the fabric of the dreamscape with her awareness and see the eternal space of nothingness that lived beyond it. Indeed, she discovered it was all within her.

No longer consumed by isolation, Jane remembered she was an aspect of all things, a divine spark of creation having a fleeting human experience—she entered the dimension of Heaven and committed herself to her soul's ancient path of astrology.

The Eternal Ocean of Light would beam glimpses of truth into Jane's perception of the sky, inviting her to question everything she'd ever believed. Jane's mission as a soul was specific to the stars—it was her path to reveal where the Anunnaki had manipulated humanity's true connection to the wisdom of the dreamscape via the sun, moon and stars. And so, the Eternal Ocean of Light began revealing details of this subtle but destructive manipulation.

On Jane's birthday, a new friend she'd met at an astrology convention gifted her a seasonal astrological planting calendar since she knew Jane loved to garden. Jane hung the calendar on the back door of her toilet, so she could study the best days of the season to sow seeds and harvest crops. On the evening of the new moon, Jane visited the bathroom. As she sat down on her porcelain throne, she noticed her bleed had arrived. Her bleed came like clockwork every new moon. As she went about her business in the bathroom, she gazed at the astrological planting calendar. The chart displayed a wheel for that calendar year, dividing it into thirteen moons, each aligning with a different sign of the zodiac. She realised the astrological calendar could track so many aspects of natural life—when she bled, when she should plant her garden, and how each moon phase passed through the signs of the zodiac. "Why would we rule our lives according to a twelve-month calendar misaligned to the natural cycles of the moon," she asked herself.

Jane's logical mind could not find a good reason for the twelve-month model, as hard as she tried to grapple for one. She pushed the question to the back of her mind and continued on with her day.

Jane was being shown, piece by piece, the true fabric of the dreamscape reality she lived within. The Anunnaki had hijacked the consciousness of almost all of humanity, even those living within the dimension of Heaven, to perceive their Earth realm as permanent physical mass rather than the dreamscape it truly was. This aspect of Anunnaki manipulation was so subtly woven into the psyche of all men, women and children of the dreamscape, it would be the final veil of lies to lift from the lens of perception of the collective consciousness. It was Jane's soul mission to assist in the lifting of this veil.

The Anunnaki were master manipulators. They had a talent for presenting lies as the truth and imprisoning soul consciousness. All souls within the dreamscape would awaken to their limitless true nature and become uncontrollable free beings when they knew the true nature of the dreamscape—a dream. The Anunnaki, with an understanding of the dreamscape's true nature, flooded the psyche of the masses with the idea that the dream was in fact real. This perceived essence of "realness" was their greatest weapon for manipulation.

Free and unbound consciousness knew there was no such thing as linear time nor space—since all things were simply an expression of the Eternal Ocean of Light—eternal beingness with no beginning and no end. So, the more "real" the Anunnaki subtly presented the concepts of linear time and space, the more imprisoned would be the consciousness of humanity.

It was easy to present linear time as a true construct, since the dreamscape realm appeared to be moving through a series of days and nights, one following the other. However, the more connected to the eternal nature of self each human being became, the more the concept of linear time eroded and a sense that all of time was indeed happening NOW felt true.

The Eternal Ocean of Light knew that as humanity awakened to their true nature, they would disconnect from the concept of linear time and fulfil their mission in the eternal now. However, the Great Mother, in all her compassion, organised into the skies a dreamscape calendar which would help her children to navigate their unique journeys of forgetting and remembering their eternal true nature. The dreamscape calendar was spectacularly beautiful, as were all things the Great Mother created. And her intention was to decorate the skies with a roadmap of knowledge for navigating life in the realm of physicality.

The Great Mother birthed two glowing balls of light that would dance around one another in the sky. One ball was bright, consistent, strong and penetrative. It was named the Sun and its essence was masculine, a perfect mirror of the cyclical nature of every man incarnated within the dreamscape. The Sun would mark the dawning and ending of every day, ceaselessly. The other ball of light was named the Moon. The Moon's light had a cool essence, and its presence transformed day by day in the night sky, completing a full cycle of transformation in one lunar month, a perfect mirror of the cyclical nature of the women incarnated within the dreamscape.

The Great Mother birthed these two beautiful balls of light, masculine and feminine, into the sky to assist her children in tracking the cycles of the days and months and to navigate the challenges of incarnation. The frequency from each light ball was potent, intended as sacred medicine for the children of the dreamscape, assisting them in their missions.

Perhaps the Great Mother's most spectacular feat of creation were the stars in the night sky. She perfected a light show of breathtaking beauty for her children to admire and study. She arranged these spectacular lights into a precisely organised network of information, intending for them to be easily deciphered, with the extracted wisdom passed down from generation to generation. As each soul was born into a new incarnation, their time and date of birth in the linear time construct could be mapped within the star network, so that every new baby born could be handed a blueprint of guidance for the mission of their incarnation written by the Great Mother herself. The Great Mother's star system was her greatest gift to her children. The information within the specific arrangement and location of each star in the night sky revealed every piece of wisdom her children needed to navigate the linear time construct with grace, until the moment they no longer needed any linear time reference and awakened to the eternal nature of reality beyond time.

Like the sun and the moon, the arrangement of the stars in the night sky too had its own cyclical nature of rotation. The sun, the moon and the stars together formed a perfectly synchronistic calendar to track, guide and mirror all aspects of natural life in the dreamscape. All humanity needed to do to receive the wisdom of the skies was be outside and bear witness to it.

Such simplicity lived within the Great Mother's creation. In simplicity, she birthed perfection. To prevent humanity from remembering its infinite power, the Anunnaki simply needed to trick human beings into believing their reality was complex. So they wove complex lies about the sky into the psyches of all men, women and children.

The Anunnaki created a concept called "space". An idea of a linear space in the sky that separated each light—the sun, moon and every star—by a degree of linear separation from Earth. Separation was the opposite of oneness, and thus concepts founded upon the idea of separation through the linear space construct were of paramount importance to the Anunnaki plan.

In educational centres for the children of the dreamscape, the Anunnaki devised lessons that would program young minds into the idea of linear space separation. They presented the sun as a ball of fire ninety-three million miles away, and they presented the moon as a ball of rock two hundred and forty thousand miles away. They presented the stars as balls of glowing mass, with linear space separating them from the Earth by varying degrees. The Anunnaki-infiltrated teachers trained the children to believe that the Earth was a ball of mass, physical and dense to its core, and that the ball of physical mass spun and flew through the space of the sky.

When the infiltrated minds of human beings gazed up at the sky, unconsciously, subtly programmed by the disempowering Anunnaki plan, they perceived themselves alone in a vast and unknown realm of physical matter called the universe.

Alone in the universe, separated by vast physical space, navigating a supposed planet of density and physical matter—humanity perceived themselves as nothing more than helpless bugs living on a ball of mass throttling through open space at speed.

The Anunnaki subtly integrated this belief system into the collective's psyche, so people rarely discussed or challenged it. The information was simply fact, fully integrated with the deepest layers of perception about the nature of reality.

As Jane continued to study astrology and connect with the vast ocean of oneness that existed within her own heart, the lies of the Anunnaki fiction unravelled rapidly from the fabric of her being. Her common sense spoke to her, piercing holes in the complexities of the Anunnaki lies at the centre point of her astronomy studies. She smiled when she considered the simple perfection of the sun and moon as they danced in the sky, identical in size, opposite in nature. And laughed at the ludicrousness of the deception she previously believed.

Common sense questions peeled back veil after veil from her perception. If the sun is so far away from the Earth casting such light, why is space presented as blackness? If the moon and sun are so vastly different in nature and positioning within linear space, why do they appear of identical size in our sky? If we are indeed on a planetary ball of mass throttling through space, why do the same star constellations appear, night after night, year after year?

Forever the critical thinker, Jane could answer each of her questions with a response she'd learned through her studies in astronomy. However, she no longer believed any of her own answers. The pulse of something simple was moving through her, offering one eternal answer—it's all a dream of divinely orchestrated perfection—it's all so simple.

One afternoon in the depths of her meditation, journeying through the vastness of the inner spaces of her heart, a burst of brilliant crystalline light exploded like an eternal firework through Jane's vision. Then, the voice of the Eternal Ocean of Light greeted her. It said to her clearly, "Jane, the lights you see are simply lights, no more and no less real than the light you are experiencing now. Welcome to the dreamscape, my child."

And with that message, Jane suddenly grasped the magnitude of the deception that had infiltrated the entire concept of the planets, the sky, the stars, the sun and the moon. She saw it all as nothing more than a set of lies devised to prevent humanity from awakening in the dream. It was all a dream, and suddenly she was consciously living out her incarnation with eyes fully opened to the miracle of incarnation—she was awake in the dreamscape.

Chapter Eighteen

I will get back to the tale of the Sacred Seven and their journey within the dreamscape shortly. But first, it feels relevant for me to share another tale of my own.

Have you ever noticed that the most profound shifts that take place in our lives occur within just a single moment? Like a chance meeting that opens a series of doorways to a life you could have never imagined. Serendipitous encounters that collapse old timelines and make way for something brand new. It's these single moments in time that we remember—captured as screenshots by our consciousness—marker points in the book of life that pin the closing of one chapter and the opening of another.

These catalytic moments don't just usher in manifest physical change in our lives; they are the moments that elevate our frequency and rapidly peel back veils of illusion. A moment for the soul comparable to a factory reset. A moment comparable to flicking the switch off on what was and then back on, minus the bugs and viruses.

Toad was one of those marker points for my husband, Scott. Toad medicine, or Bufo, came to us in 2024 in Bali.

We encountered a medicine man who introduced us to 5-MeO-DMT, the sacrament of toad, described by some as the most powerful psychedelic on Earth, and we felt a strong calling to experience a private ceremony. To Scott and me, Bufo was the last frontier in our journey with plant (and amphibian) medicine. We were afraid of its intensity—a thirty-minute psychedelic journey to obliterate the false sense of self and meet infinite consciousness. Understandably, we had our reservations.

The ceremony itself was one of the most beautiful moments Scott and I have shared as a couple. Scott went first. A long and steady pull on an unfamiliar apparatus to draw in as much smoke as possible, followed by an exhale of effortless dissolution that melts your body and mind into utter surrender. In a Bufo ceremony, the word surrender takes on new meaning. You have no choice but to let go—you cannot fight against anything—you cannot cling to any fragment of control. I witnessed Scott's body collapse back onto the mattress with his exhale of the smoke. As his muscles twitched and eyelids fluttered, I saw his conscious self dissolve. I knew he was in profoundly capable hands, and I sat, watching on, silently sending him waves of love from my heart—a prayer of protection to keep my beloved husband safe.

The medicine man was exquisite to watch in his craft. His chants, his drumming, the movements of his hands—it was a practiced dance of energetic alchemy for the Bufo realms—and he was clearly a master of his craft. After twenty minutes, I could see the flickering of Scott's eyelids smooth into conscious blinks. I watched him become reaware of the room and his surroundings. Tears were streaming down his cheeks, and his chest and belly vibrated with his gentle cries. His eyes were wet with emotion. I watched as he looked at the medicine man in utter admiration and gratitude. "Wow, wow, wow, wow. I have no words," Scott muttered as he moved his hands about his face, hair and body as though he was checking that all the pieces of his physicality were in place. He brought his hands together at his heart in a gesture of gratitude and thanked the medicine man repeatedly as tears continued to roll down his cheeks.

When Scott finally sat up, he was still shaking his head in disbelief. "I literally became oneness and vibration," he told me as I waited patiently for his insights into the experience. He described to me a pure realm of nothingness—absolute white light with no beginning and no end. "I went to a realm of complete oneness, and I was it." Still bewildered, laughing and crying in astonishment, Scott spent the next few minutes slowly trying to find the right words to explain his journey, but he struggled. "You're going to love it, babe."

After my experience of a vastly different nature, Scott and I left the ceremony space, jumped on our motorbike and headed to our favourite cafe, Alchemy, for a cacao and an integrating debrief before picking the kids up from their kindergarten.

The following morning was business as usual—the chaos and precision of the well-oiled routine that prepares two children under six for their day at school. On the way to school, we dropped into our favourite cafe again for a couple of coconut milk lattes and a fruit bowl for the kids. But something had flipped in Scott. He became irritable and frustrated with me and the children for no apparent reason. It appeared he wasn't coping, as if the space within the cafe and the quiet chatter was thumping through his head causing him to spin into a vortex of confusion.

"Are you okay, babe?" I asked him with immense concern.

"I've gotta get out of here," he told me. And before I could even check in with him, he had hopped onto his motorcycle and taken off. He had never taken off on me and the kids before. I knew instantly that something was seriously wrong. I quickly finished my coffee, hurried the kids onto my bike, took them to kindergarten and then raced home on my own as quickly as I could to get to Scott.

When I arrived back at our villa, Scott was sitting on a beanbag next to the pool with a look of absolute agony on his face. I'd never seen him like this before. He was hurting, and his face was clenched with his pain. He looked afraid. "As I was driving home, I didn't know who I was," he whispered to me. The vulnerability in his words touched my heart, and I kneeled beside him, hugging him tightly and holding his head to my chest. "When I was driving, I could have just let go of the handlebars and drifted off to die," he continued. He was completely ungrounded. The Bufo had exploded his consciousness so widely open that he had met himself as pure oneness, shattering his need to exist in the realm of physicality. "What is the point of all this?" he asked me, looking around at his surroundings, shattered by the sudden pointlessness of his existence.

I remember saying something to this effect: "Just let me work with your energy for a bit. Don't overthink this, or look too far into the future. I'm going to serve you some hapeh." Hapeh is a sacred medicine of the tobacco plant served through a snuff pipe called a tepi. When Scott spent six weeks in Peru sitting Ayahuasca with the Shipibo shamans, he developed a relationship with hapeh for its profound grounding properties.

Scott pulled himself upright to sit cross-legged at the edge of his beanbag, waiting for me to serve him the medicine. Before I did, I held the tepi to my heart and prayed. I prayed to my guidance system, Scott's guidance system and the guidance systems of our children. I prayed with utter devotion for help to bring my beloved husband back into his body so that he can live out his human experience with meaning, joy and purpose. An immense wave of energy flooded through me, opening my heart. At that moment, I moved into a complete trust of Scott's experience. There was not a single thing to worry about—he had just moved through a monumental spiritual upgrade. And all he had to do to integrate it was fall in love with Pachamama, Mother Earth, once again. I guided one end of the tepi towards his left nostril, and with the love of Pachamama riding my breath, I blew on the tepi, shooting the tobacco snuff into Scott's nose. He winced with the initial intensity and then exhaled with an audible sigh that seemed to relax his whole body. After a minute, I served him again, this time into his right nostril. Again he winced and then sighed into an even deeper release. I tiptoed to the back of his body, and something guided me to place my hands on his sacrum. I spoke silent prayers of the Earth and Scott's grounding into his hips and his base.

Then, I waited patiently for him to return from his meditation with the medicine.

After ten minutes, Scott opened his eyes and looked at me with a smile. He began laughing. Through his chuckles, he looked around the villa, at the pool, the kitchen and our belongings. "What is the point in all of this?" he said again, although this time with a tone that brought a vastly different meaning. He laughed, and I laughed with him.

"I don't fucking know," I replied. We continued giggling like children who had become aware that we were playing one hilarious game of life.

"I guess we'd better just have a good time then?" Scott concluded.

"Absolutely," I agreed.

Now, let's get back to the tale of the dreamscape and delve further into the story of the Sacred Seven. So far you have met Dario, Anna, Jerry and Jane. The fifth divine dreamscape soul of the Sacred Seven was a woman named Beth. Please read on.

Chapter Nineteen

The dreamscape was birthed as a playground of remembering. A paradise for the taking, should each soul choose to experience it as such. Of course, in order for a human soul to recognise a paradise, it would need to have some kind of inherent knowledge of what the opposite of a paradise was. In order for beauty to be recognised in one's surroundings, a wisdom of the meaning of ugliness would need to be held within the fabric of one's consciousness. And thus, the Anunnaki's presence within the dreamscape had a purpose. Their reign of terror within the fear-based matrix gifted each human being with the wisdom of what it meant to live a life built upon the essence of destruction. From this inherent wisdom, gifted by the Anunnaki presence, each human being could feel and recognise a life built upon the bountiful essence of organic creation. And since each human being was birthed from that same bountiful essence, each human soul would recognise its true nature, mirrored back to them through the external beauty of a life birthed from organic creation.

The Eternal Ocean of Light and the Great Mother knew of the wonderful gift the Anunnaki infiltration actually was. But once each human soul had gained the wisdom of destruction versus creation, anti-life ugliness versus organic beauty, the Anunnaki served no purpose within the dreamscape that could assist in each soul's sacred mission of remembering their eternal nature.

You see, many human beings believed that the Earth that they lived upon was a physical planet, floating in physical space that required a dual nature in order to exist. However, the Anunnaki infiltrated this concept, distorting humanity's understanding of what duality truly entailed.

To create balance within the dreamscape, the Great Mother birthed two types of humans—men and women, opposite in nature, but both in the name of love. She birthed the sun and the moon, the days and the nights, summer and winter, joy and sorrow, death and birth. But all of these opposite forms were birthed in the name of love. Even death, a loving liberation of a tired physical body retiring, liberating a soul into its boundless rest phase in the cycle of reincarnation. In this respect, of course, the dreamscape had a dual nature but one overruling consistency—everything was birthed in the name of love. The Anunnaki was formed through the multiplication of anti-life matter, like the pus that drips from an abscess or a malignant tumour that multiplies. The Anunnaki was not birthed from love, it was formed from anti-life matter—a fear frequency. Thus, the presence of the Anunnaki within the dreamscape was not an aspect of its organic dual nature. The Anunnaki infiltration was inorganic, and once each human soul had awakened the innate wisdom within that recognises pure organic creation both externally and within themselves, the Anunnaki would need to be rid from the dreamscape.

Since the inception of the dreamscape, the Eternal Ocean of Light had simply watched on as each soul initially forgot their eternal nature and then went on a lifetime-long journey of remembering. The Eternal Ocean of Light had witnessed the struggle of this journey and the balance of energy within the dreamscape at times tip towards the fear-based paradigm of no return.

It was always the Eternal Ocean of Light's intention to liberate the soul from its cycles of incarnation once it had accessed the dimension of life within that dreamscape that was Heaven within a single incarnation. However, watching on, the Eternal Ocean of Light witnessed a potential for a different outcome for fully realised souls and the dreamscape itself. The Eternal Ocean of Light had created the dreamscape experiment to watch the journey of souls forgetting and remembering. But a curiosity developed, and the Eternal Ocean of Light pondered.

What if the dreamscape rebirthed itself into a realm of physicality for souls to simply be their eternal true nature?

The Eternal Ocean of Light continued pondering.

If every soul had remembered its true nature, what would their existence within a realm of beauty and wonder look like? If every soul lived within the dimension of Heaven within the dreamscape, what would they create? How would they work together in harmony in an earthly paradise?

As these questions danced through the consciousness of the Eternal Ocean of Light, the frequency of contemplation spontaneously birthed six different species of uniquely powerful light-beings—similar to the Andromedans, but with distinct features and frequencies.

The Eternal Ocean of Light had pondered over a utopia, a paradise for beings to live out their existence knowing themselves as aspects of the eternal one, and in the pondering had birthed six different species of light-beings and their own realms to exist within. The energy of contemplation had manifested six new realms into form, each with its own birthing energy of creation. Each new realm birthed had its own Great Mother and unique species of light-being that inhabited it. The six new realms were vastly different in design from the original Earth dreamscape, since a sky dotted with sparkling lights to assist in the navigation of linear time or a moon of monthly lunar cycles was redundant. Not bound by space or time, the six new realms were limitless. The skies of each of the new realms were open, vast empty planes of their own description.

The new species of beings that inhabited the realms were light, not dense in physicality but holographic mirages taking near human shape. Since each new being, regardless of the species, knew itself as the Eternal Ocean of Light, they couldn't densify their form into physical mass. Instead, they glimmered as translucent light, sparkling with their unique frequencies.

Each realm and the beings within it gave themselves different names based upon their unique frequencies. And the languages these beings spoke were not languages at all but pure sound frequencies expressed. Since pure sound frequency cannot be densified into letters, a human being couldn't write or spell the names of the realms and the methods of communication expressed within them. However, some human souls within the dreamscape who had activated their ability to see beyond the spectrum of visible light could connect with these beings, see their realms, and speak their sound frequencies.

Because of the distorted programming fed into the human collective psyche around the stars in the sky, many human souls had an innate awareness of other beings and realms beyond the dreamscape but perceived these realms and beings to be intertwined with the notion of the stars and their existence within linear space. False ideas misled the masses into believing that other beings and realms existed in the sky's vastness, which they perceived as physical space, separated by millions of kilometres. But creation birthed a dreamscape, which was nothing more than a dream, a playground for remembering, not physical in nature but a multidimensional hologram for learning the eternal nature of self.

The Anunnaki's speciality in deception was half-truths. They would subtly feed the masses with information about other realms and beings, but would deceive humanity into believing that contact with these beings existed outside of themselves, and even outside of the Earth realm.

All realms existed parallel to one another, and the way to intercept another realm was simply through vibration. The Anunnaki had intercepted the dreamscape by aligning themselves with any pulse of fear present within the human collective. And human beings could intercept and connect with any parallel realm of their choosing simply by altering their frequency.

Each realm dreamed into existence by the Eternal Ocean of Light had a unique essence—a divine frequency. And even though language couldn't fully describe each realm's frequency, I will define them as follows to share this tale: the Sirian realm, the Lyran realm, the Arcturian realm, the Pleiadian realm, the Orion realm and the Ashtar realm. In these realms and in the Andromedan realm, despite subtle energetic nuances, there was a common thread: love. In each realm—love simply was.

Each of these realms was a paradise of its own description, although the Earth dreamscape was the only realm that could have it all. The Eternal Ocean of Light asked the beings of each realm to assist the human beings of Earth to wake up to their true eternal nature. The Eternal Ocean of Light called upon the unique frequencies of each group of beings to guide individual human souls in whatever way they could, hoping one day, each human soul would realise and activate these divine frequencies within their own physical body and collectively birth a new dreamscape—a dreamscape free from the Anunnaki, protected by each human soul's unwavering pulse of love.

The Eternal Ocean of Light was ready to begin a new experiment—to witness the miracle of existence within a rebirthed dreamscape anchored in the dimension of Heaven. And through the Sacred Seven, a plan was being formulated by the Great Mother to ensure this rebirth took place before the energetic tipping point of no return in the linear time year of 2041.

Beth was one of the Sacred Seven, a uniquely extraordinary woman who was in direct contact with non-human beings beyond the visible light spectrum. Beth could see these luminous light-beings with her eyes open or closed, and she could receive messages from them via her consciousness, delivered as crystal clear audible thought forms.

Beth dedicated her life to her connection with these beings, and although she had awakened to her limitless true nature, she still perceived these beings to inhabit physical planets in space. Each evening, Beth would sit on the balcony of her apartment and gaze up at the night sky. Since childhood, she had felt she didn't belong. She saw lunacy everywhere she looked in the day-to-day life of the surrounding society that was perceived to be normal. From her school desk, Beth's mind would wander off, out the classroom window into the clouds and the trees. She had always struggled to build friendships and felt a lack of resonance and genuine connection with almost everyone around her. But when she sat on her balcony and gazed up at the night stars, she felt a sense of home.

When her eyes were closed, Beth would receive visions of realms where advanced civilizations of crystalline light-beings would live in radical harmony with one another. Her consciousness showed her a holographic shimmering realm of stone-looking temples with majestic water fountains flowing into crystal shallow pools for prayer, where the humanoid beings wore jewels, gold and decadent fabrics. She saw a realm tinted with a hue of blue, where the humanoid beings were tall with hands twice as big as their heads. In this blue realm, she saw glass temples of unfathomable decadence that reached high into an unfamiliar sky that stretched beyond sight.

Although Beth struggled to navigate her life within the dreamscape, she never felt alone because she was connected to an incomparable pulse of love and beauty from the moment she closed her eyes. Beth felt more at home in these alternate realms than she did in her own Earth realm. When she became hyper-aware of the fear-based matrix existing around her and the heinous acts of hate and greed human beings committed against one another, Beth would pray to be freed from Earth. She'd look up at the stars from her balcony and plead with the stars to be rescued. She ached to be brought home to a realm anchored in loving harmony.

The more Beth prayed to be liberated from Earth to experience life in an alternate realm, the more pain she felt in her existence within the dreamscape. Her resistance to life on the Earth realm was a weight of suffering she was unconsciously feeding through her desire to be rescued.

From her inner-city apartment, she perceived a growing, deafening madness all around her—the neon lights of billboards, the honking of traffic, the continual white noise of inorganic internet frequencies. She had to escape. And since she couldn't escape Earth entirely, she removed herself from the city and moved into a quaint farm cottage set upon four hundred acres a five-hour drive from the city. Other than the farm owners, who lived in another cottage on the far side of the property, Beth was alone. She moved all her work as a multidimensional healer online and confined herself to a life of solitude—just her and the wide open sky.

The Great Mother watched on as Beth suffered in her solitude. She'd found freedom from the madness of the city, but she hadn't liberated herself from her discontentment with the earthly dreamscape itself. Light-beings of parallel realms were created to assist humanity; however, Beth needed another frequency of energetic help to liberate her from her suffering. The Great Mother knew the best place Beth could connect with this frequency was on the sacred lands of Pachamama. Thus, the Great Mother intentionally guided her to this specific farm.

When the Eternal Ocean of Light dreamed forth the dreamscape, with the sky, moon, stars, sun, oceans and lands, each aspect had its unique energy and a unique spirit of wisdom. Earth—the land, grass, soil, mountains, rivers, great oceans and vast plains—all of this had a spirit, a wisdom. And this spirit was called Pachamama.

The Great Mother had guided Beth, unbeknownst to her, to a sacred land so that she could reconnect with Pachamama and remember not her eternal nature, since that she already knew, but her primal connection with her reason for existence within a realm of physicality.

During the long summer days on the farm, Beth would explore. The farm had a creek that meandered through it, dotted with ancient redwood trees. During long walks, Beth would delight in watching the playfulness of squirrels darting from tree to tree. Beth fell in love with one particular tree that cast a perfectly sized shadow for respite from the sun, allowing dappled rays to warm her shoulders whilst she rested at the bank of the creek.

On one particular day, Beth packed a large water flask, a warm jar of ceremonial cacao, her favourite handmade mug, a picnic rug and her journal into a bag intending to spend a few sacred hours under her tree. There was an eerie magic about the day. The sky was overcast, although it wasn't cold. The trees were still; no wind blew, and the humidity dampened the soil beneath her as she walked. When Beth arrived at the tree, she felt exhausted, overcome with a heaviness that forced her to lie down. She laid out her rug and relaxed flat on her back with her knees bent up and her bare feet planted in the soil. As she softened deeply into the rug, with the warmth of the summer earth beneath her, she delighted in the pleasure of the soil between her toes.

She moved her feet, side to side, digging them deeper into the soil, lost in the subtle sensations of every minute rock, fallen leaf and blade of grass that interacted with her skin. Tired, she fell into a meditative state of sensory pleasure—stimulated simply by the feeling of the soil on her feet. Her breath deepened. And as her feet rhythmically pressed into the Earth, Beth moved her hips and thighs, gyrating her pelvis in harmony with the sensations of the soil under her feet. She felt overcome with a simple pleasure. It wasn't a sexual pleasure; it was too rooted in innocence. It wasn't erotic; it was primal. The pleasure of just being, in her body, with the soil. Aware of the moment and her experience, Beth giggled at the simplicity of her joy. She bunched up the rug with her hands and scooped it towards her body so that her hands too could touch the soil on either side of her. And Beth lay blissfully alive on her back, her knees bent up, with both hands and feet wiggling and pressing into the surrounding soil.

She felt connected to something she'd never felt before—a moment of radical aliveness in her body. She was consciously aware of her experience, and yet fully merged with it. For the first time in her life, she didn't want to escape the Earth; she wanted to merge with it. As Beth's breath deepened, the intensity built in the pleasure she was experiencing. Her thighs began trembling—a tremor that spread into her hips and her yoni. The energy was so strong, Beth let out a groan of immeasurable pleasure. The trembling continued up her spine, into her throat and her tongue. Her whole body was vibrating with aliveness, and as Beth moaned with the primal intensity bouncing up her body, the energy became uncontrollable. She had no choice but to let go completely. The vibrating intensity continued into her tongue, and with her body bouncing and vibrating on her rug, a strange language of incomprehensible speed exploded from her mouth. Her tongue and jaw were moving at a rapid pace, and to Beth, it felt as though the Earth itself was speaking through her. And it was.

Pachamama had arrived in Beth's body, and Beth had surrendered herself to receive a most sacred rite of passage—the activation of her primal light body—her kundalini. Pachamama danced through Beth's body, opening her to experience pleasure and aliveness through every cell of her physicality. Beth's fingertips came alive with pleasure. Her thighs felt as though they held the power and grace of the ocean within them. She felt the frequency of the stars in her back, dancing aliveness up her spine. It was a full-body orgasm of infinite proportions. With her body still vibrating and pulsing, her psychic vision flashed into something new. She wasn't just seeing through her mind's eye—she was the vision—her whole body activated with psychic sight. She could see that the land she rested upon wasn't separate from her; it was her. The ancient redwood guarding her space, no longer just a tree, but an ancient brother from a shared home.

She was home. Pachamama was her home, and for the first time, she'd arrived.

From that moment on, Beth was no longer obsessed with alternate realms, and she no longer looked to the stars for salvation. She found contentment in her being. The present moment came alive with the beauty that surrounded her on the land. Beth continued to meditate and pray, but she felt the wisdom of Pachamama speaking through her most. Her sacred activation under the ancient redwood aligned Beth to the frequency of her mission and her reason for incarnation.

The Great Mother whispered guidance to her. The solitude of the farm no longer served her. But equally, it no longer served the Eternal Ocean of Light's greater mission. The dreamscape would rebirth itself, and Beth had been handed the key for its labour and delivery.

The plan for the dreamscape rebirth was simple—the activated human body vessel would alchemize the dreamscape into a new paradigm of Heaven for each awakened soul to relish together in the pleasure of physicality, anchored in the frequency of love.

The activated human body vessel, when anchored in love, was such a potent energy transmuter that one human being in their light body could alchemize any amount of fear back to love effortlessly. Collectively, an army of activated human body vessels, anchored in their light body, could alchemize the fear of the entire dreamscape and the Anunnaki with it.

In this alchemical process, all fear-based frequencies would be exposed—a collective exorcism of infinite proportions.

Humanity was being prepared, guided lovingly by the Great Mother to activate their body vessels through their connection to Pachamama and they were being guided to free themselves from all resonance with the fear-based frequencies woven through the dreamscape by the Anunnaki. Humanity was being guided to heal traumas, lift veils of deception and remember their eternal true nature, so that as clear and activated human beings of the dreamscape, they would be ready to serve as a collective army of energy transmuters for the great rebirth.

The Eternal Ocean of Light and the Great Mother, in their infinite wisdom, saw the linear time year of 2041 as a pivotal marker point for humanity and the dreamscape. If enough human beings became activated and ready for the great collective rebirth, the Anunnaki would have no chance. In the year 2041, the catalytic benefits of the Anunnaki presence would cease, and their plan for absolute domination over the human soul would come into full effect. In the linear time years leading up to 2041, their nefarious plan darkened, with a plot to exterminate the soul and completely enslave the consciousness of humanity. But as the plan darkened, humanity awakened. The timing was a delicate balance, but with the ceaseless help of light-beings of alternate realms, the Great Mother, Pachamama and the Eternal Ocean of Light itself—the most spectacular liberation of humanity and the dreamscape was indeed possible.

Chapter Twenty

It's me again—just briefly interjecting the tale of the dreamscape with a musing I simply cannot keep to myself. It seems we are indeed living in the dreamscape. What I am writing no longer feels fictional. When I first sat down to write these tales, they spoke through me; they glided from my consciousness onto the keyboard as I typed. Nothing I share with you has come from any kind of methodical planning. It has just arisen spontaneously, like my fingers can't type fast enough. As I write, I don't know what the next paragraph or even the next sentence will be, and yet, it takes shape, opening my eyes to a clearer vision.

As I write this now, it is the year 2025. And if the tales of the dreamscape were indeed true, then in only sixteen years, we would arrive at some kind of energetic tipping point. And yet, as I gaze out of my writer's window, with the wisteria vine dangling from the patio outside, it does all seem rather far-fetched. Could there really be people so evil living amongst us they are not even human beings but some kind of anti-life frequency trying to destroy humanity? Surely not. And yet, when I think back to moments in my work as a healer, I have seen demons being released from the wombs of the traumatised, and every day I witness evil at play in the world around me. Far-fetched? Perhaps not.

I do not know a single person who relishes the thought of war. And yet, year after year, war goes on—atrocities are committed, homes and hearts are destroyed. So who is creating these wars? It certainly isn't my neighbour, a former colleague of mine or a mutual friend. It's someone foreign to me. Someone whose inner mechanisms of thought I cannot understand. And yet, war goes on. So this leaves me wondering, are the people devising wars and orchestrating evil people at all? Or are they some kind of foreign being to this Earth?

If the tale of the dreamscape reveals in even some minute detail a way to exterminate foreign evil from the Earth, I'm curious. A world without evil is something you and I have never known, and yet, it is what feels most natural to me, and I'm sure to you too.

I do indeed notice a kind of distorted plan to eliminate the human spirit racing towards a frightening finish line. An artificial intelligence that can rid us of the mundane sounds promising, but artificial intelligence that appears to be attempting to form intimate relations with the psyche of the collective feels concerning. I see small children sitting in the trolley, being pushed around the supermarket, mesmerised and hypnotised by the bright flashing screen of their mother's phone. I recently went to Perth, the closest city to us here in Margaret River, and as I waited with seven strangers for my coffee at a trendy city-fringe cafe, no one looked up—not one person. All of my fellow takeaway coffee drinkers stood, black screen in hand, head hung forward from their necks as though they would dive into the phone completely if given the option. As I looked around the coffee shop at the decor, I felt like the odd one out, like I was living in a world where casually looking around the room was a peculiar thing to do.

If there were a nefarious plan to rid humanity of their connection to the Divine by robbing them of their soul—the black screen of the smartphone could be a good way to do it. They are so addictive! And our entire lives, from banking to movies to shopping, exist within them. You can even cultivate and maintain social or romantic relationships via the little black screen. And the more we look at the screen, the more the screen shows us what we love to see. For me, it's advertising for spiritual courses on one app, and videos about hacking consciousness on another. All of it appears to be light and expansive, and yet it all pulls me into the black screen.

Only a handful of times have I felt a sense of connection to anything other than the black screen when looking at my phone. I did once find a business coach from an Instagram ad that I believed to be divinely guided; I did not search to find it—I opened my phone and bang, there it was, and with it, a knowing within my body. But more often than not, it's like we binge scroll to feel something, some sense of connection, and as we do, we receive a dopamine hit that brings nothing more than an insatiable desire to keep scrolling. I know what it is to feel Spirit move within me, and I have never felt it from the depths of a scroll session with my phone.

I have cultivated a conscious awareness of the addictive nature of the phone. I am sure you have too. But for those who have not yet developed such conscious awareness, when do they know to put the phone down and start living? From what I observed at the coffee shop, many people are not living. I don't know about you, but I feel connected to Spirit most when I am in nature, exploring creative passions, with my family or, obviously, doing intentional spiritual work.

If a nefarious agenda to sever humanity from their souls was being carried out, then distracting human beings from their organic state of aliveness by keeping their awareness trapped in a programmable device seems like a legitimate path of execution.

In the coffee shop, it was merely a mundane moment that could be filled by replying to messages, watching a little video or whatever it may be. But in my reality, it was a moment lost. Chance encounters missed. A stranger's smile that never came. So if, like the tale of the dreamscape describes, there is an infinitely intelligent power orchestrating miracles for us day by day so that we can live our most beautiful lives, how could we ever feel the guidance of that intelligence when our consciousness is being harvested by a little black screen.

In an alternative reality, at the moment in the coffee shop, I would have stood on the checkout counter and yelled,

"Put your fucking phones down or you're all going to die!" Maybe that would have been a strong enough message for them to look up for a moment. After gaining their attention, if I explained about evil beings foreign to the Earth trying to harvest their consciousness, I wonder how many of them would have kept listening? Maybe half? Maybe just a couple? I'm sure at least one or two would just look back down at their phones—even if I made the announcement naked. But in this alternate scenario, I'm guessing one of the seven would have wanted to know more, and to that inquisitive soul, I would have passed them a book detailing the tales of the dreamscape. It would be that inquisitive soul that might wake up to their true nature and follow their innate guidance system, leading them towards a life of freedom and joy. Perhaps it would be that soul who could help in the great rebirth, as described in the tale of the dreamscape.

My heart rejoices and overflows with love when I think of the courageous leaders who have stood on the soapboxes of their own platforms shouting to the masses about the hidden evil on the Earth. David Icke is a name that comes to mind when I think of such courage. The ridicule he encountered while trying to awaken the masses should have destroyed his soul, but he is clearly guided and protected, and his soul is an unshakable light, guiding so many in humanity. What a legend.

There are countless courageous leaders across the Earth at this time, exposing hidden evil. Some expose the evil hiding behind government and finance. Healers too are exposing the hidden evil hiding within the bodies and minds of the collective by exposing entities and demons and alchemizing them through love. Exposing evil, both in the physical world and Shamanic realms, takes courage. I have learned through my path as a healer that the demon is alchemized when the observer feels no fear in its presence. When the healer exposes the entity and stares into the root of its existence, seeing its true form as nothing more than fear, love destroys it. But of course, this takes courage, because seeing a demon can initially trigger fear just as seeing the evil of the world can trigger fear.

It feels to me now that all fear-based frequency on Earth is being exposed. Evil governments and politicians are being exposed. Demonic entities are being exposed. Hidden trauma patterns are being exposed. The evil behind inverted systems of medicine and education are being exposed. It's all coming out of the shadows for humanity to witness. And as piece by piece, all that was hidden is revealed, every fragment of fear within each of us, individually, will be exposed from the hidden shadows of self. These are the places within where the hidden evil of the Earth has penetrated the energy body.

So before I return to the tale of the dreamscape, I would love to offer you the piece of wisdom that has allowed me to face some of the most heinous demons of the spirit realm whilst keeping my heart open. Why? Because as these demons are exposed, we all have a role to play in destroying them. And if there is even a fragment of truth in the tale of the dreamscape, perhaps we all need to prepare ourselves as fearless energy transmuters who can collectively rebirth a new Earth.

Remember, demons are just fear frequencies—whether you can see them, feel them or just know their presence is near. It's an unsettling fear-based energy that disturbs the room and disrupts the palpable pulse of your own nervous system. All fear is alchemized by love and you are love. In the face of fear, do not fear your own fear. Just allow. Do not run, fight or try to push anything away. Do not even try to transform the energy—you are the love that alchemizes all things. Just be the love that you are. Breathe into and from your heart, as though your chest has its own nostrils to breathe from. And regardless of what you feel or see or sense, keep your heart open. Close your eyes and feel the perfection of your existence—your body, your breath, your divinity, and then by contrast you will feel the warped frequency of the demon, however it presents. When you recognise the distortion, you will see its powerlessness. And from an open heart you can command the single sentence that will alchemize a fear-based entity in an instant, "I SEE YOU."

Chapter Twenty-One

The tale of the dreamscape continues.

Following the innate whispers of guidance that spoke through her, Beth left the farm and moved to a bustling new town on the outskirts of the city. The town's high street was alive with boutique artisan shops and eclectic cafes. It was a buzzing hive of aliveness that appeared to welcome all expressions of the human experience. After a full year isolated on the farm, Beth fell in love with people-watching. She found a new favourite cafe where she could pull up a stool at a high table beside the window and gaze out at the adjacent sidewalk watching the full spectrum of humanity walk by—the serious, the free-spirited, the artsy, the corporate, mothers, grandmothers, the wealthy and the destitute. Although at times Beth craved the solitude of a life connected to the land, she welcomed a new essence of connectivity that wove through her days as she encountered the warmth of strange smiles and spontaneous conversations in shops and cafes.

Beth had cultivated a new way of offering her healing gifts to the world. Rather than channelling her multi-dimensional healing through online sessions, Beth had devised a method to connect people to the energy of Pachamama, to bring this energy up through the body, clearing trauma and releasing blockages. Her innate guidance system showed her how to help others experience the same full-body kundalini activation she received under the ancient redwood. She'd been guided away from solitude, back to community, to facilitate these activations for as many people as she could.

Her favourite cafe was a central point of connectivity within the community. A huge pin-up board was affixed to the wall next to the coffee pickup counter, and from it hung flyers of a vast spectrum of workshops. As Beth pinned a flyer for her upcoming event, Pachamama Life Force Activation Workshop, another flyer caught her eye. It was an electric blue, A3 flyer strategically placed in the centre of the board. Full Spectrum Quantum DNA Repair with Jerry was the title of the event, and the computer-generated image in the flyer's background was of blue light-beings with a luminous glowing aura. As Beth studied the flyer, flushes of energy tingled around the crown of her head, spreading into the back of her neck, and flooding down her spine. She closed her eyes, and in her usual way, asked her guidance system for confirmation. "Am I to attend this event?" she enquired. The response was a whispered yes from within her consciousness and a more intensified flood of tingling energy down her arms, creating goose bumps. Beth scanned the QR code on the flyer and purchased tickets to the event for the following evening.

The event was held in a conference room within a five-star hotel in the city. When Beth arrived, the event's magnitude and scale shocked her. Volunteers wearing lanyards greeted the crowds, scanning tickets and directing them through the double doors into the dimly lit space of the conference room. "This guy is obviously a big deal," Beth thought to herself. Beth checked in with one volunteer and found her seat; Row 27, Seat Q, her ticket read. As Beth settled into her chair, she gazed around the room and estimated a capacity of upwards of five hundred people within the space. The energy was humming with the soft chatter of the people and the collective anticipation of an evening of mystery and healing magic.

Amidst the stage lighting, Jerry finally appeared. Like a humble superstar of healing, he walked out onto the stage and took his place on a stool next to a podium, front and centre. Beth gazed in awe at his powerful presence that commanded the room. The room fell silent, and Jerry hadn't even spoken a word. He simply sat with hundreds of people awaiting his direction and closed his eyes. His unspoken command rippled through the conference room, and everyone, including Beth, closed their eyes too.

Beth was sensitive to even the most subtle frequencies, and the moment she closed her eyes, her body began vibrating. She wasn't sure what Jerry was doing up there on the stage, but she could feel a frequency of powerful healing already moving through her body. Beth fell into a deep meditative trance and allowed the waves of energy to flush through her cells. It felt beautiful to her—like a familiar grace that reminded her of her connection with beings of alternate realms she'd spent so much of her life attuning to. She felt a sense of home within her body—reconnected to a multidimensional aspect of herself she'd completely forgotten.

Her eyes peeled open just slightly, and through her squint she saw that the entire room was awash with a blue hue. She saw giant light-beings with long fingers and luminous auras moving through the room, pushing waves of encoded crystalline energy like lightning bolts into people's bodies whilst they vibrated in entranced hypnosis. Beth could see it all so clearly. She knew this realm. It was the same realm she'd visited with her eyes closed many times in the past—only this time, her eyes were open and the beings were intercepting her reality, walking amongst the people.

Although Beth was consciously aware in the space, as she looked around, she noticed everyone else was in a deep trance with no conscious awareness. It was as though the other participants were sleeping and she was awake within their dream. Suddenly, a force jolted Beth's body to stand up—and so she did. With her body standing upright whilst the rest of the room remained seated in deep trance, Beth was unsure what was happening to her. An unseen force of profound power that she was not in control of had moved her body to stand! Her body was moving of its own accord, beyond her conscious control. But Beth was not afraid. She knew what it was to fully surrender to loving energy and trusted implicitly that she was being moved by love. There was a mighty current moving Beth, and of course she could have fought it, in the same way a rowing boat can paddle upstream, but instead, Beth gave herself to the flow of the current. She allowed the energy to move her, trusting that her body was being guided along a sacred path.

She walked her body, step by step, as though in slow motion, past the seats of the people in her row, and up the centre aisle towards the front stage. Her mind flashed with the thought of the strangeness of what she was doing, but she trusted she was being moved by the same energy that was facilitating a miraculous healing of an unexplainable magnitude. She sauntered through the blue mist that wafted down the central aisle, as though the pace of her gait was in complete sync with the tremors of each person's collective vibration and each pulse of crystalline healing light that danced through the room. Her body was being moved, inexplicably, in harmony with the frequency of the room and the incredible light-beings within it.

Beth arrived at the stage, and, one step at a time, her body walked her up to stand directly in front of Jerry. The moment she stood before him, he opened his eyes and gazed into hers. Beth darted her gaze to the side and saw that next to her stood another woman, of a similar age to her, in the same dreamlike trance state that must have guided her too to walk up. Without any conscious choice, Beth had found herself standing at the front and centre of the stage beside Jerry and the other woman who stood beside him.

The powerful force continued to direct Beth's body, and without thought or approval from Jerry, she turned to face the crowd, who were still deep in an altered state of trance, unaware of her sudden appearance on the stage in front of them. Beth's hands moved like the conductor of an orchestra, reaching into the depths of the earth, waking up the dormant energy of the land beneath the conference room. The blue-beings were still present within the space; however, Beth was orchestrating the energy of the room. Her hands were alive with the power and grace of Pachamama. With effortless and thoughtless might, Beth guided the spirit of Pachamama up into the seat of every chair in the room. Like an ancient vine of pure aliveness that grew from the roots of the earth under every chair, Beth conducted the energy up and into the base of the spine of everyone in attendance. One by one, people's eyes blinked open. They became aware but still deeply connected. The frequency of the room changed, and a pulse of pleasure vibrated up from the ground through the legs and hips of each person. "Breathe and make some sound," Beth commanded. As the first spoken words of the event landed into the cellular knowing of all in attendance, a primal moan of the collective weaved through the space, transforming the room from a multidimensional light temple into a primal cave of aliveness and remembering. As each participant surrendered to the inconceivable power of Pachamama rising through their bodies, cries erupted, primal roars sounded and many collapsed from their chairs onto the floor so that their bodies could move and roll freely with the primal aliveness moving through them. The room was awash in both grace and chaos. The grace of Pachamama held each person in a womb of unseen safety, as stored chaos and distortion released from their bodies in waves of primal sound. The power of Pachamama and each person's own innate life force was clearing lifetimes of stored trauma through the portals of their throats via sacred sounds of liberation.

Beth stood, surrendering to the power that moved her—her focused gaze unwavering and her delicate arms conducting with all the might and power of a giant. She took the room, deeper and deeper within. And suddenly the room went grey. A distorted frequency of fear pulsed through Beth's body, and she became afraid. She closed her eyes and breathed into her heart. Her mind wanted to race to concern, but she knew better. She knew the sheer magnitude of love and depth of healing within the space had exposed the demonic frequencies that had been secretly harbouring within the bodies and psyches of the collective group. The Anunnaki infiltration within each person was exposed to such a degree that Beth could see it.

Jerry took Beth's hand and whispered to her, "Do not be afraid." And with those words of affirmation, the other woman who had been guided by trance up to the stage erupted in the most exquisite song of harmonic perfection. It was Anna. Like an angel, with an unbound capacity to access the most divine notes of vibrational song, Anna poured her heart through her voice and wove crystalline sounds into the room that danced like light through the fabric of fear. Her song was medicine for the distortion in the space, and the grey fog of fear dissipated into clarity. But an eerie post-traumatic fear still lingered, as the people rested on the floor and in their chairs, semi-entranced and silently bewildered.

The fear hadn't left completely. It was still there. And although Anna's song had assisted, something sinister still lingered within the space. Jerry took Anna's hand too, and the three of them stood, without words, instantly knowing the next course of action. They closed their eyes and prayed for help. Anna called upon the Great Mother and the Eternal Ocean of Light, who she'd come to know so intimately through Kirtan and Ayahuasca. Beth called upon Pachamama and the beings of light who had always assisted her in the past. And Jerry called upon all of it—he asked for help of the highest order. He prayed, "Guide us to alchemize this fear into love so that everyone in this room can be liberated—free, whole, one."

A tiny woman stood up suddenly from within the audience. She was no more than five feet but with the courage of a lion. Beth, Anna and Jerry watched on, in radical trust that this woman of tiny stature was the answer to their prayers.

Anna resumed her angelic song. Beth continued to conduct the spirit of Pachamama through the room with her hands and spoke somatic guidance for breath and sound release to the audience. Jerry closed his eyes and called upon the blue beings of light to resume their healing through the space. All aspects collided to create something monumentally beautiful. The room transformed into a glowing sun of radical light—blinding to the eyes and euphoric to the body. And at the centre of the room, within the white light, a demon appeared. Like a discordant mass of moving tar, the demon wriggled and squirmed—it snarled and it laughed. The audience couldn't see it. They were deep within their own processes of energetic release and repair. But through their work, Beth and Anna saw it. And in his mind's eye, Jerry saw the creature too. The tiny woman walked towards the demon, who squirmed and fidgeted with discomfort in her presence. The demon was four times the size of the woman, and yet it appeared to be afraid. Gazing into its black, lifeless eyes, the tiny woman stood before the demon. Like a lion, she felt no fear of the demon, but compassion. As she gazed into the depths of the jerking entity, her heart opened with love.

"How awful it must be to be void of soul," she whispered to the demon. "How awful it must be to be the manifestation of trauma and pain," she continued. With every word, her chest expanded as the energy of love lifted and radiated from her physical heart. "I cannot fear you because I see you. I see what you are. I see what you've manifested from. And I feel your powerlessness." The tiny woman closed her eyes for a moment and breathed slowly into her heart, cultivating a love palpable throughout the entire room. Her physical body flickered into light as the Lyran beings of courage merged with her body. Her head flashed between forms—that of a white lion and that of a delicate human woman. As light, she expanded, and the Lyran beings flooded her with the same courageous love that they did David in his battle against Goliath. The Lyrans readied her. And with her readiness, she opened her eyes and gazed into the depths of the deep blackness of the demon's stare. With crisp certainty and ferociously loving courage, she commanded to the demon, "I see you." And with that, the demon vanished into a spark of light, and the frequency of the room lifted to that of a summer's day—fresh, bright and reborn.

Anna's song changed from angelic tones of an infinite crystalline nature; she grounded her voice in a familiar song from her childhood. "This little light of mine, I'm gonna let it shine. This little light of mine, I'm gonna let it shine." As her song echoed waves of joy through the room, the participants awoke fully from a healing that would transform their lives forever. They were free from Anunnaki infiltration within their bodies and they were connected to the eternal truth of their nature and the primal gifts of their incarnation within the dreamscape. The smiles of the audience showed their recognition of an experience so profound it was unexplainable. And to cut through any attempt at mental analysis, Anna invited them to sing with her.

Five hundred voices of joy sounded through the space. "Let it shine, let it shine, let it shine," they chorused. Those who'd released lifetimes of ancestral grief and pain, stood themselves up from the floor, and like children, began swaying their bodies with the innocence of their song. Fathers, mothers, grandmothers, grandfathers, sisters, brothers, daughters and sons—together, they sang, they swayed, and they laughed playfully.

Dario, the young British war veteran who had fallen in love with Anna at the Ayahuasca retreat, rushed to stand by her side. In awe of his beloved and her power as a songstress, he wrapped his arm around her and pulled her in close. "You are phenomenal," he whispered in her ear.

It was 2036 in the linear time construct of the dreamscape, and five members of the Sacred Seven—Jerry, Anna, Beth, Dario and Grace, the tiny woman with the courage of a lion—had received the blueprint from the Eternal Ocean of Light and the Great Mother to rebirth the dreamscape and rid it of the Anunnaki presence once and for all.

Chapter Twenty-Two

Now let's continue delving all the way into the depths of the dreamscape tale, to uncover the fate of the Sacred Seven in their mission to liberate humanity from the grip of the Anunnaki once and for all. So far, I've introduced you to six of the Sacred Seven.

As Jerry, Anna, Beth, Grace and Dario connected over an unforgettable co-creation of miraculous healing, Jane, the astronomer turned astrologer, was diligently pursuing her own sacred mission.

Jane had a gift—a divine fusion between her brilliant mind and her psychic gifts. Jane served humanity from all countries of the dreamscape through online Vedic astrology readings. Through her devoted study of the precise art of astrology, she could pinpoint moments of significance in a soul's incarnation in relation to the fulfilment of its sacred mission. Jane could read precise years, months and even days in the linear time construct where a person could radically ascend into a higher dimension of existence. Whenever Jane read someone's chart, she would extract moments of significance and note them down on paper. For each notable moment of significance, Jane would close her eyes and place the tip of her index finger over the written date as though her finger could open a visionary portal in her mind's eye that reveals a complete picture of the potentiality of that moment in time. It was a potentiality and not an absolute, since Jane knew that each human being that came to see her for a reading had been granted the power of free will.

It was Jane's remarkable gift, bestowed upon her by the Eternal Ocean of Light, that extracted the visionary insight into Jerry's future that she shared with him via email. Jane had a strong intuitive urge to ask Jerry for his birth time and date at the close of the event in Dubai when they had met. And after reading his chart, she saw clearly a window of time in the year 2041 where Jerry would conduct a mass healing at the magnitude of a filled stadium.

Jane remained committed in her practice of meditation. It was no arduous task for her to meditate. Meditation was the most cherished moment of her day since it was where she could receive messages from the Great Mother, detailing specific insights into her mission and her path ahead. The Great Mother had told Jane of the importance of her unique readings. Her astrological and psychic insights activated something sacred within each person who received them—vision. It was vision that sparked the innate essence of creation that moved through every human soul. All human creativity started with vision. Every human being had the Great Mother's power of creation, and all they needed to do to activate that creative power was to envision their most sacred desires. Envisioning was each human beings key to creation.

When Jane shared an insight into what was possible for someone's future, a bright pictorial spark would ignite within their minds, projecting into their own holographic dreamscape reality a frequency of creation. From that creation frequency—completely aligned with their soul mission, as written in the stars—the full force of the Great Mother would move through them, opening doorways of opportunities and shattering limitations by any means necessary.

To be specific, Jane's mission was to ignite the spark of vision that aligned each person she served with the highest potential outcome for their incarnation. The Great Mother would then orchestrate the rest. All a human being needed to do to experience the fully realised vision as described by Jane was bend their free will to the will of the Great Mother and the Eternal Ocean of Light.

So, when Jane emailed Jerry explaining that he would perform a mass healing in a stadium, a spark of creative excitement activated within him. After receiving Jane's email, Jerry attuned himself daily to the frequency of his inevitable success. Unwavering certainty replaced his doubts. He aligned himself on his path so acutely, envisioning his highest potential with radical clarity, and thus he thrust forward at momentous speed towards that inevitability.

His events grew rapidly in attendees. His name became known and his face became recognisable throughout the dreamscape in all dimensions. Jerry was portrayed as a science-denying lunatic, and his methods were described as dangerous through the Anunnaki-controlled mass media. The Anunnaki were afraid of leaders like Jerry. He was the orchestrator of a powerful force that was a poisonous virus to the existence of the Anunnaki—love.

Together, Jerry, Anna, Beth, Grace and Dario combined forces and continued to facilitate the spontaneous multi-faceted healing that they orchestrated together on the day they first met. Each of them played a significant role. Jerry was the name and the face. He drew in sizable crowds that continued to grow as the five of them travelled the world relentlessly, bringing their multidimensional healing to all corners of the dreamscape. Jerry's commanding presence effortlessly captured large groups of people's awareness, guiding them into an altered trance state where their logical minds were sedated. The soundscapes that Anna graciously created with her voice resonated with realms of pure love, allowing a vibration of softness and beauty to flow through a space, even in the darkest moments of healing. Between Jerry and Anna, miraculous subtle DNA healing took place, nervous systems were reset, and nefarious unconscious programs of the mind were unhooked. Following this subtle work, where the conference room of each event would flood with a familiar blue hue whilst light-beings of alternate realms assisted in miraculous ways, Beth and Grace would then combine forces.

By calling upon Pachamama, and guiding people to somatically breathe and release sacred sounds of liberation,

Beth's work unravelled residual trauma from deep within the body, opening the channel of the body for the innate primal life-force energy to activate. Beth's work guided people so deeply into their unloved aspects that it often exposed the Anunnaki infiltration at the root of the traumatic contraction. It was at this point of each healing that Grace, the delicate woman with lionlike courage, would flood the fear-based demonic frequency with courageous love, destroying it instantaneously.

Dario also contributed substantially—he was the grounded support that each of the four healers needed. Jerry, Anna, Beth and Grace could enter a trance-like state of healing for others so deeply, they'd forget where their shoes were, or they'd forget to drink water. In all of those moments, Dario was there. Dario was attuned to each of them, and also to the entire experience. As the events grew, Dario would speak with sound and lighting technicians, organise volunteers and ensure that every logistical detail was taken care of. Without him, it was impossible. Dario knew the power of the work of his beloved Anna alongside the other three, and he was so honoured to fulfil his mission in devoted service to them and the greater mission. His life had taken him so deeply into the realms of horrific trauma that the fear-based matrix had nearly killed him. And his life had elevated him to the realms of bliss and liberation, where he'd met the love of his life and connected to a divine and intelligent energy that was guiding him every step of the way. Dario didn't need to be the star of the show. He had arrived at his dimension of Heaven and was moved to tears of gratitude every time another healing event he supported drew to a finish.

The group of five found an extraordinary rhythm and flow in working together. As experienced healers of their own unique crafts, Jerry, Anna, Beth and Grace found a profound ease in their organic collaboration they'd never experienced working by themselves. They didn't need to plan—it was as though everything was divinely taken care of—and it was. There was a wave of momentum carrying them forward collectively, and all they needed to do was surrender to its current.

The plan to rid the dreamscape of the Anunnaki by the energetic tipping point of 2041 was in full effect. The Great Mother and the Eternal Ocean of Light were orchestrating a mass purge of the Anunnaki infiltration at all levels. More than ever, souls were being called to rise to fulfil their sacred missions as healers. Armies of healers were called into action across the dreamscape to assist humanity in purging the demonic hooks internally bound to unresolved traumas, perpetuating fear-based falsities in their psyche.

Of course, the Anunnaki had infiltrated every aspect of human life, as well as the inner mechanisms of the human psyche. However, ridding the Anunnaki from all levels of human society, such as systems of medicine, education, media, government and finance, was a secondary and far easier task than humanity's internal purge. This was because, once humanity was freed from its internal trauma-based bondage to the Anunnaki, its perception of the world around would transform into that of truth, and all decision-making processes on a personal level would choose to disentangle from false, fear-based systems, making them redundant. And thus, intuitively led armies of healers were the most effective weapon against the Anunnaki. A collective of human souls anchored in love, liberated from fear-based trauma imprints, was an unenslavable population of free beings. And all new systems birthed by a free population were built upon love, with the collective withdrawal of participation in the old fear-based systems being enough to crumble them.

And so, the Great Mother and the Eternal Ocean of Light infused the gifted team—Anna, Beth, Grace, Jerry and Dario—with an energy of support and protection that guided them miraculously. Within two years of working together, they had moved their events to wide, expansive fields out in nature, guarded by trees, to accommodate more people. Like a music festival of sacred stillness, campers, one to two thousand in number, would drive to remote locations to experience the renownedly popular event named Surrender. The group had called the experience Surrender since they never knew what was going to happen and the entire concept had created itself! And thus, Surrender felt an apt name for the five of them, and an accurate description of what the participants could expect when purchasing their tickets.

Moving the healing events out onto sacred land only strengthened the phenomenal power of the healing frequency that moved through the facilitators and the participants. When the large gatherings of people melted into the altered trance state of deep healing and the beings of light arrived to assist, waves of palpable energy emanated vast distances into the surroundings, weaving into the homes, cars, shops and workplaces of the communities in the far distance. The larger the Surrender events grew in scale, the more exponential the shock waves of secondary healing sounded through the surroundings. In one town, the group would facilitate group mass healings, freeing two thousand souls from ancestral trauma and reactivating them into their sacred human light bodies, and in another country, a child would spontaneously purge a demonic infiltration in its sleep. The secondary healing wave that emanated from the power of each event cast its own healing web throughout the whole dreamscape—so powerful were these events.

And so the Great Mother and the Eternal Ocean of Light continued to bring more people to each subsequent event. The five were guided across the dreamscape; through Europe, Asia, Australia, North America and South America. And everywhere they went, they were serendipitously guided to a peaceful, sacred place on Pachamama, where the healing would be most amplified. Without effort, one spontaneous encounter after another showed them exactly where to go. The lands of Pachamama throughout the dreamscape were dotted with energetic vortex points that could magnify the frequency of healing and open portals to higher alternate realms for assistance. The five were directed to farms, forests and fields that aligned with these vortex points.

Each event was a complete rebirth for all in attendance, and secondarily, a profound healing for hundreds of thousands across the entire realm. Each time, the construct of linear time would pause, the logical mind of each participant would stop—and everyone in attendance would dissolve into an altered dreamlike state with no beginning and no end. There, they would meet the Eternal Ocean of Light and themselves in their true and limitless form. At that point, their DNA would be repaired, allowing their energetic and physical bodies to heal. Then their limitless consciousness would be guided back into their activated light body to reconnect with the loving truth of Pachamama and their incarnation.

The healing for each individual in attendance was absolute, and the tidal wave of passive healing subsequently beamed through the collective was of monumental significance.

The five healers continued their work, year in, year out, and the events continued to multiply exponentially in magnitude and impact.

Of course, the Anunnaki controllers who had been hiding within the shadows of the dreamscape noticed these shockwaves of profoundly healing frequencies blasting across the realm. They felt the gaping cracks in their grip of control and scrambled to devise a plan to eliminate the events and the five who facilitated them.

In the linear time year of 2039, the Surrender events were a known phenomenon, dreamscape wide. And the healing frequencies of the events were having a notable impact on the human collective. Each time the five facilitated an event on a sacred vortex of Pachamama's wide open lands, a crystalline explosion of blue light rippled into the vast reach of the dreamscape for all to see and feel.

Masses of human souls were awakening to their true nature at a momentous rate. Parents began withholding their children from school attendance, as they became aware of the distorted programs being purposely fed into the psyches of the innocent. Sales of poisonous drugs plummeted, as humanity awoke the dormant DNA that catalysed spontaneous self-healing. The hidden infiltration of the Anunnaki became known to many. As psychic gifts activated collectively, many could clearly see distorted non-human beings inhabiting the bodies of politicians and leaders. The Anunnaki were no longer hidden, their nefarious plans became incredibly obvious. Following their soul mission, many human beings began fearlessly speaking out against the Anunnaki presence within the dreamscape. The distorted fear frequencies behind television, entertainment and music were palpable to a collective attuned to harmony. So en masse, humanity turned away from this form of infiltrated entertainment.

Masses of human souls aligned to their limitless creative potential. There was a surge in new expressions of art, healing, music, architecture, medicine, food and education. Community markets appeared in every town where activated human beings gathered to share in their newly found creative expressions. Communities came together to delight in music and dance whilst relishing in bountiful harvests of homegrown food and creatively inspired textiles, furniture, clothing and art. The people turned away from consumption and back to shared expression.

All that didn't align with truth was abandoned, en masse. Collective trust in the government eroded almost completely, since truth as a frequency was anchoring into the bodies of so many of the people. Awakened human beings abandoned their black screens and stopped engaging with the digital number currency as a form of economy. New local economies spontaneously arose, built upon creative exchange and tangible resources.

The Great Mother and Eternal Ocean of Light witnessed as the seed of potential for a reborn dreamscape germinated to show signs of something spectacularly harmonious and beautiful. 2039 in the linear time construct marked a turning point for a new way of life in the dreamscape—radically anchored in truth.

But, the Anunnaki were not ready to give up control. Many of their weapons for manipulation were compromised. So many human souls had stopped listening to the infiltrated mass media and had stopped consuming the hidden poisons of mass produced food and weaponised medicine. Their plan for empathy erosion was failing, since many were no longer interested in watching movies showcasing bloody murder for entertainment. Humanity had re-found community, and thus many were instead spending their evenings sharing in food and music. Anunnaki infiltrated music was abandoned. Very few were interested in listening to recorded distorted frequency via the black devise—they were creating their own music with their families and neighbours and relishing in the pure joy and simplicity of their own sounds, attuned to their own lives. Humanity's free will had chosen the path of truth, and there was nothing the Anunnaki could do about that fact.

However, there was something the Anunnaki could still control, although this time, it wouldn't be from the shadows. Their plan for dreamscape domination from behind the shadows was not working, and thus their ultimate plan was for obvious obliteration of the human soul in full sight.

Since so much of humanity was making decisions for themselves in alignment with the Great Mother and choosing to liberate themselves from fear, both internally and externally, the only way the Anunnaki would hold on to control of power was by weaponising frequency against the free will of human beings. The Anunnaki knew this would be seen as outright war, and after an obvious manoeuvre to destroy the soul of human beings, there would be no blindsided complacency from the ones they controlled. Just a slave class and a ruling class, where both knew their place and despised the other. This would leave the Anunnaki, as the ruling species, very susceptible to being overthrown by the collective force of those they controlled. However, it was their last remaining plan. Control from the shadows leading to docile complacency and illusory free will of the enslaved was no longer an option. Outright frequency war was all they had left. As anti-life beings formed from decay, there was nothing for them in their own realm. They had nothing left to lose, and the power of the limitless spirit of the human collective to gain.

The only beings the Anunnaki had on their side were the ones still, against all odds, completely entrenched in the fear-based matrix, imprisoned by their logical minds, bound by the constructs of linear space and time, with no concept of their infinite nature. Some of these fear-based beings had been so deeply infiltrated by the Anunnaki that in the year 2040, they were completely dis-ensouled. These soulless human beings were no longer human at all. Many of these beings found positions of power within the military, since most industries had collapsed. Despite a collapse in many distorted systems of the dreamscape, the military was the largest it had ever been. This physical force was the only power the Anunnaki could exert over the growingly aware human population.

The dreamscape-wide military police force was called NATO or the Non-human Anunnaki Terrorist Organisation. In 2040, the presence of NATO strengthened in communities and peaceful family neighbourhoods. Tanks would patrol neighbourhood streets, with non-human officers wielding guns and flying spy-drones into gardens and through the open windows of homes. The goal of this intensive military force was simply to evoke fear once more through the populace. Where there was fear, the collective could be controlled and thus the Anunnaki assumed this relentless display of authoritarian power to evoke such fear.

However, the vast majority of human beings had remembered their true nature. They knew they were love, quite simply, in their essence. The thought of death didn't terrorise them, since death was the ultimate liberation—leaving the dream and returning to truth. And thus, even the prospect of death didn't scare the awakened human collective. There was no outcome worse than living in fear, and thus feeling fear was not a choice they gave themselves. They chose love.

As the year of 2040 progressed, the Anunnaki weaponised the skies at full force. It was the last weapon they had at their disposal, since again, even the fully awakened human being couldn't impose their own free will to change the sky—it was simply out of their reach. Through telephone towers, the Anunnaki tuned an audible frequency through the airwaves intended to congeal the blood and disrupt the nervous system. The sound turned on violently, shocking every human being with its deafening screech, making them immediately fall to the ground covering their ears. The NATO officers were given specialised earmuffs to protect themselves from the discordant sound blasting from the towers at every street corner.

When Anna felt the vibration of the frequency attack through her body, she dropped to the floor in violent convulsions and momentarily lost consciousness. As she fell into a sleep, she heard an angelic voice sing through her. It reminded her of the opera she'd once sung in choir as a child, although this song filled her with light. When she opened her eyes, she could no longer hear the frequency attack—just a gentle ringing in her ears, which passed within a few minutes. The light-being guardians of the dreamscape began beaming songs of harmonic balance in complete resonance with the activated human body vessel through the inner mechanisms of every human being. And the Anunnaki attack lasted only moments, since it was utterly counteracted by an extraordinarily high sound frequency of unmatched power.

And so, NATO was the only chance the Anunnaki had to reign supreme over the dreamscape. NATO was directed to break up community gatherings and ensure no trade of crafts, foods or arts was permitted. Human beings were forced to retreat into their homes and gardens. For ten months, human beings across the entire dreamscape were policed by a draconian martial law that didn't allow them to leave their homes at all. Powdered food was airdropped by drones into houses through opened windows. The water supply leading into each home was poisoned by a sedative chemical to subdue the imprisoned human beings into a nonresistant dull haze.

However, the light-beings of alternate realms moved their crystalline frequency through the water pipes, negating the power of the chemicals and enriching the water with the necessary minerals and vitamins to sustain optimum vitality to assists the human collective in their great time of need.

With absolutely nothing to do and nowhere to go, the awakened humanity went into a ten-month vipassana of silent prayer and meditation. Never before had the collective human spirit been more attuned to the whispers of the Great Mother and the Eternal Ocean of Light. Every day, the Great Mother's children, confined to the walls of their homes, guarded by pure evil on the streets outside, sat and attuned to the limitless loving energy of their creator. Fear had not taken over. The human souls knew who they were as pure loving expressions of the Eternal Ocean of Light. And thus, they knew the NATO military patrolling the streets had no power.

Into the psyche of every human soul imprisoned in their home, the Great Mother spoke the same message. Over and over, she repeated the message until every man, woman and child had received it. She gave them a date—9th September 2041—and she told them to be prepared.

And so, they waited, Jerry, Anna, Beth, Grace, Dario, and the rest of the human collective—meditating, praying and consciously choosing to remain anchored in love, confined to their homes, until the Great Mother would speak to them again, instructing them exactly what to do next.

Jane the astrologer, restricted to her home, received the date in meditation and psychically attuned to its significance. It was written in the stars and she had seen two possible outcomes. The dreamscape was closing in on an astrological choice point—fear or love. The 9th of September would either mark humanity's end, or humanity's beginning.

Chapter Twenty-Three

Across every corner of the dreamscape, the strong NATO military presence obliterated the construct of society as it was once known. Confined to their homes, the human beings of the dreamscape could not work in their usual ways. Jane stopped offering online readings for a fee since no one could pay. Her internet provider made Beth's online healings impossible. They cut off her connection when her account fell into arrears. Anna, Beth, Grace and Jerry, who had become publicly known, were banned from posting online and promoting themselves, and the Surrender events came to an abrupt halt.

The illusory economic system of digital numbers on the screen collapsed, since very few were earning or spending money. Shops and restaurants didn't just close; they became desolate.

In the past, the Anunnaki had closed shops and restaurants, forcing people to stay in their homes, but this was different. In the past, people had stayed connected online, educating themselves and discerning truth through information. They had formed political movements of rebellion to oppose Anunnaki tyranny. But this time, the internet was a prison of its own description. Information wasn't free to access. Everything was censored by the online NATO presence, and if a post, email or private piece of writing on the computer was deemed inappropriate, online access was blocked. And thus, the people of the dreamscape experienced complete isolation from one another. They couldn't see one another in person or online.

The awakened human beings knew better than to eat the powdered mixture airdropped to them via NATO drones. The Great Mother guided them to drink water simply, although it had become a known fact that the water pumped into people's homes through the public water service was compromised—intentionally poisoned by the Anunnaki. However, the light-beings of alternative realms ceaselessly purified and activated the water, transforming what was once poison into a comprehensively nutritional, healing source of nourishment. The light-beings alchemized the tap water into a healing elixir. The Great Mother guided her children to pray to the water daily and to receive each sip with the intention of fuelling the body with limitless crystalline magic.

The NATO firing drones destroyed any self-sustaining food source accessible in people's gardens. They obliterated veggie patches, fruit trees and even backyard egg-laying hens. For ten months, the awakened human beings of the dreamscape fasted from food as they knew it—relying completely on the water accessed via the taps in their kitchen. When the Great Mother told them to trust the water, they did, and they noticed that despite not having access to food, they grew strong day by day. After ten months of fasting and ingesting nothing more than activated water, the awakened human beings became light in form. The density of their physical bodies altered into something completely new.

Families living together noticed their loved ones gradually becoming slightly translucent. When one person stood in front of a light-filled window, another could see the sun's emanating rays shining through their body. When husbands and wives made love, they didn't just merge carnally; they experienced their bodies and consciousness merging completely as one. The ten-month dreamscape-wide journey of devoted prayer and fasting was radically altering the fabric of the human collective.

By the tenth month, many human beings had activated the ability to communicate telepathically with one another. Since they cut off internet providers and policed technology access, awakened human beings mastered telepathic message sending via conscious thought-form and received messages as audible words spoken internally, along with a visionary insight that spontaneously appeared in their minds. Despite being separated physically, the human collective was more connected than ever. It was as though the restrictions of linear space had dissolved. Awakened human beings were connecting with the Eternal Ocean of Light through prayer in each moment, and thus, they were connecting to the essence of oneness that united them collectively. They were no longer separate. Through the

Anunnaki's attempt to isolate the human collective, they had united many into the truth of their eternal oneness.

The 9th of September 2041 arrived. Around one hundred million NATO military officers patrolled every street in tanks, wielding machine guns and remotely operating spy drones capable of firing ammunition at great distances. The Anunnaki controllers, the families of interbred bloodlines who had been hiding in the shadows, sat in their finely appointed manor homes watching live footage of the ground patrol operation broadcast to giant screens in their libraries. There were twelve key Anunnaki families, each with their own private estate hidden by miles of inaccessible forest. The twelve estates interconnected via an ultra-high-speed underground railway network. And on the 9th of September—the execution day for an irrevocable step in their plan—the interbred non-human controllers watched the outcome via live footage.

The Anunnaki controllers were satisfied with the outcome of their plan thus far. There had been minimal pushback from the human populace, who they assumed had been frightened into submission, remaining in their homes awaiting command. The ten-month home detention plan was to evoke crippling fear throughout the human collective—making them susceptible to frequency attack and weakening them into a voluntary relinquishing of their own power. With access to the wisdom encoded in the star system of the Great Mother, the Anunnaki controllers selected the specific date in September, recognising a potential choice point for humanity that could enable an absolute dreamscape takeover.

The dark plan was simple. Broadcast instructions would be sounded throughout the dreamscape, directing each person to leave their homes, step out onto the streets and kneel in submission to the authority of NATO. This kneeling would signal to the Anunnaki controllers the absolute acquiescence of the populace and the voluntary surrendering of their free will to them.

A sudden eruption of sound began—bellowing sirens echoed across the dreamscape. And the bitter voices of the patrol commanders of every neighbourhood directed all 1.5 billion human beings to step out of their homes onto the streets of every village and city of every country across the dreamscape. For some, the sun was rising; for others, it was the middle of the night. But the switch of an intercontinental alert system was suddenly turned on to full volume.

Of the 1.5 billion people, nine hundred million activated their light-bodies, possessed crystalline DNA, and had access to the full spectrum of their innate human powers bestowed upon them at birth by the Great Mother.

The other six hundred million were neither activated human light-beings nor so utterly infiltrated by the Anunnaki that they were void of soul—they existed in the dimensional space in between. They had not alchemized their own fears or followed the ceaseless guidance of the Great Mother showing them the path to liberation. These six hundred million chose independently and freely what they had always perceived to be easy—a life that doesn't question the way things are. Of course, this group had felt fear during their ten-month detention; however, their compliant thoughts, words and actions granted them unfiltered access to the internet—an infinite pool of distraction and entertainment to dull their internal suffering.

Since this group didn't listen to the whispers of the Great Mother, they ingested the airdropped powdered food, which negated the healing frequencies woven through the water supply. And instead of crystallising into their light bodies, they densified into hardened physical form. Their cells thickened. Tumours, hardened fatty deposits and blood clots formed through their physical bodies. They were vulnerable to the consistent frequency attacks sounded through telephone towers that the activated human beings had become immune to.

And when the 9th of September arrived, although nine hundred million human beings had transformed radically into crystalline light-beings, the other six hundred million had decayed into fear-based human mass, where their soul was still somewhat present but its infinite power was being harvested for the gain of the Anunnaki controllers.

The speakers sounded down the streets and instructed the entire human population to leave their homes and step out onto the sidewalks. The awakened ones had received explicit instructions from the Great Mother. She had whispered to them all, "Go out onto the streets, but do not kneel."

As the sirens sounded their deafening screech, the human beings of the dreamscape followed the NATO military directions and left their homes for the first time in ten months.

When Jerry stepped out of his Texas home, the glare of the sun blinded his eyes, and he felt himself move into a surrendered state of absolute trust in the miracle of the moment that was unfolding. As he looked to either side, he saw many of his neighbours radiating a crystalline glow of joy that cast an auric eminence all around their bodies. He saw that so many of the people who lived on his street had transformed. Their bodies looked taller, their hearts beamed a vibrant pulse of positivity, and faced with tanks and non-human patrollers with blackened eyes, they appeared peaceful and unfazed.

Dario and Anna stepped out of their California home, and the swirling sounds of the perpetual sirens dissipated into a background hum—all they could hear was the chatter of their neighbours overjoyed to see one another after ten long months of separation. As they gazed around the adjoining front gardens of their home, it was as though the people did not even notice the tanks; their joy of reconnection was so overwhelming.

In Germany, apartment blocks dotted the homes on Jane's densely populated street. She noticed two distinct dimensions overlapping one another. She heard the quiet echoes of a NATO military officer yelling at her to get on her knees. But despite the officer being a mere meter from her, she could barely hear his commands. He was so close to her and yet of no consequence. She remained standing and silently watched as several people dropped to their knees in frightened acquiescence of the NATO demands. The people who knelt seemed grey, as if their life force had been drained. They submitted, bowed their heads, and bound their hands behind their backs voluntarily, as though they were cuffed but they were not. Enraged, the officers continued yelling; despite that, Jane could barely make out the content of their muffled demands. Instead, she heard a tone, a vibration wave that danced down her street. It was a song that rippled through the fabric of her body, opening her to love and reminding her of the beauty of life. Jane didn't know who was singing, but it was as though an angelic presence was standing right beside her, beaming the language of the sun, the moon and the stars through her body as a smooth rhythmic vibrational massage of infinite proportions.

On the 9th of September 2041, the Eternal Ocean of Light and the Great Mother paused time. In truth, there was no time to pause for the activated human beings. They had transcended the construct of linear time and had arrived in pure presence—with no beginning and no end. Where a song was sung in a single moment in California, it could be heard in equal measure in any moment, in every country.

In a remote town of Australia, Beth too stood outside her patrolled home and heard the same song Jane was hearing in Germany. Who was singing this song? It sounded like Anna's voice, although Beth knew Anna was in California. Beth closed her eyes and felt Anna's song ripple through her body. She smiled as she received the warm bath of loving energy that danced through her cells, vibrating with the song. On Beth's street too, tanks patrolled and officers violently commanded the people to kneel in submission; from the corner of her eye, Beth saw a handful of people drop to their knees. But not Beth; she was awash with the pure pleasure of the familiar song waves moving through her. It was as though on her street there was a nightmare surrounding her that was of no consequence to her—she stood outside her home in Heaven—alive in her own activated light body. She knew everyone had a choice and that those who had fallen to their knees had chosen their own path.

The Eternal Ocean of Light and the Great Mother were ceaseless in attempting to massage the free will of every human soul of the dreamscape onto the path of liberation. But the choice point had arrived, and those who had chosen a path of submission to evil had created their own fate. The moment six hundred million fear-led humans dropped to their knees in acquiescence to the Anunnaki was the moment the Great Mother withdrew her support and the Eternal Ocean of Light called back their souls into the realm of nothingness.

Grace was in Scotland, standing outside her home on her outer-city street. She was beaming a crystal hue of white light as echoes of chaos sounded around her. The sky was overcast and grey, but as Grace gazed up, the clouds parted, making way for the sun's rays to land on her cheeks, filling her with a warmth that spread through her body as a shower of pure joy.

Jerry knew this was his stadium moment, only the stadium wasn't a single place in linear space—it was something far bigger than that. His stadium was the dreamscape in its entirety. And all activated human beings were being called forth as participants in the event he'd been training for his entire life. Jerry closed his eyes and called upon the beings of light who had supported him in all moments of his work as a healer. But they didn't come. He waited for the street to be awash with the familiar blue hue that opened a portal of access for light-beings of alternate realms to appear—but the blue hue didn't come. He lifted his chin to the sky, opening his heart and arms in a prayer of devotion to the highest powers of healing and divine orchestration. And then he realised—he was the light-being of his realm, and so too were his neighbours who stood beside him. He smiled at the beauty of his realisation and closed his eyes to resume his prayer. "I call upon the fully activated human light-beings of the Earth," he commanded through his consciousness.

Dreamscape wide, the command of Jerry's prayer echoed through the telepathic consciousness of every activated human being—and they joined in collective silent prayer of calling themselves forward into service—one unified army of light for the rebirth of the dreamscape. Standing, Jerry reached his arms out to take the hands of his neighbours. No longer separated by linear space, simultaneously, the impulse to connect with one another wove through every village, city and country of the dreamscape. Nine hundred million fully activated light-beings of the dreamscape stood, hand to hand, weaving currents of pulsing electromagnetic frequency across the lands and oceans of Pachamama.

Together as one, the nine hundred million human bodies vibrated into a unified trance of light. The chaos of the tanks and military officers shrunk into nothing more than a fluster of scrambling ants, whilst the pulse of the unified collective intensified. Anna's angelic voice continued to weave song lines of connection through the dreamscape, as the human beings opened their hearts to a pulse of love at a magnitude never experienced.

The nine hundred million crystalline human beings merged into one unified pulse of love. Time stopped. Linear space collapsed in an explosion of quantum luminous brilliance stretching the vastness of the Eternal Ocean of Light itself. Anna, Jerry, Beth, Grace, Dario and Jane dissolved into nothingness—merged as an infinite light for a moment of immeasurable duration.

Through the body of merged light that was the awakened unified collective human consciousness, the dreamscape itself alchemized. As though the gargantuan spark of light of the unified consciousness could vacuum up all aspects of the dreamscape—like a cyclone that could draw in the cities and the buildings, uprooting them from the earth.

Nine hundred million fully crystallised human beings had unified into one singular toroidal field of consciousness for energy transmutation. A luminous doughnut-shaped sphere of pulsing light that could vacuum in discordance and rebirth harmonic perfection.

The great explosion of unified consciousness devoured the dreamscape in its existing form, purging it of evil, purifying all distortion. The infinite ball of light that was humanity's unified consciousness vacuumed all aspects of the dreamscape built upon untruth. The tanks, NATO, the willingly enslaved beings, the Anunnaki controllers hiding in their manor homes—all of it was vacuumed into the light to be alchemized by the loving force of humanity's unified consciousness. As the spark drew in more distortion, it shone brighter. The spark of light drew everything in, including the black screens, houses, roads, and government buildings. All that remained was Pachamama, Mother Earth in her purest form. The rivers, the mountains and the lakes remained; the vast open deserts and plains remained; the oceans, lands and all benevolent creatures that inhabited them remained.

Linear time ceased, and the lands and oceans repaired themselves in an instant. The coral reefs regrew in an explosion of spectacular colour. The ancient echoes of the decimated rain forests germinated fresh life, which sprouted and grew instantaneously. Where cities once stood, the truth of the lands that had been cleared spontaneously reappeared.

The dreamscape rebirthed itself into a paradise of wonder. The unified collective consciousness of light birthed its own reality into form to exist upon the healed lands of Pachamama. Nine hundred million sparks of creative genius collided to birth an entirely new Earth realm. The unified spark of collective consciousness, infused with the Great Mother's power of limitless creation, birthed great community buildings of opulent grandeur and beauty. Suddenly, the spark of limitless power erected homes for everyone, which were interwoven with their natural surroundings and alive with the pulse of Pachamama's essence. Each home was uniquely sparked into being with the qualities of beauty most resonant with the family that would inhabit it.

As collective light, they birthed a teleportation system for instantaneous travel, powered by the ether. On the healed lands of Pachamama, everything human beings could ever want or need for a life of pure peace, pleasure, and beauty was birthed into instantaneous form.

Collectively, as one, they birthed spectacular temples for shared celebration and prayers. Water fountains, ornate sculptures of the Great Mother and gargantuan crystals adorned these temples. Sacred water systems spontaneously etched into geometrically harmonic waterways, following the natural contours of Pachamama, for directing healing water effortlessly to all of humanity. Crystals of clear quartz, amethyst and agate lined these sacred waterways to mineralise and charge the water. Instantaneously, limitless harmonic energy pulsed from the sacred waterways into the surrounding ether, powering homes, buildings and teleportation systems with an ever-present frequency attuned to the vitality of all beings.

Bountiful fruit trees, berry bushes and vegetable patches sprung into existence, surrounding homes with an overflowing supply of seasonal produce. Everything human beings could need to live in radical harmony, surrounded by beauty, birthed into form.

Once the dreamscape was rebirthed, the spark of light that was humanity's unified consciousness dissipated. Each human being individualised once more. They landed in their unique new homes, with their families and loved ones, upon resonant, sacred, healed lands of Pachamama.

The activated human beings had rebirthed the dreamscape into a paradise of joy—a playground for being—with nothing to forget, and nothing to remember. The Eternal Ocean of Light and the Great Mother watched on in sheer delight, witnessing their children arrive in their collective manifestation of Heaven. The Anunnaki were gone, destroyed at the root by the ferociously loving power of humanity, which was now fully realised, creatively inspired and alive with the joy of the miracle of incarnation.

In a new Earth realm, humanity was free to simply be. Each soul knew itself as an aspect of the one and thus existed simply to relish the gift of incarnation. Linear time was gone, although the sun, moon and stars remained for their beauty alone. The moment was an infinite gift, holding within it limitless possibilities.

With no hero's journey to conquer, each human being of the new Earth realm lived in a frequency of wholeness. There was nothing more to become or even strive for. And thus, play, joy, connection and creativity became the focus of each moment.

With the new Earth realm a paradise for creativity and play, innovation accelerated. Food, music, art, architecture and transport rebirthed themselves into a more and more spectacular form with each dawning new sun. Not because an ongoing upgrade was necessary, but because pure creativity expressed itself freely through all beings and thus collectively, the new Earth paradise became an ever evolving expression of Heaven. A paradise for being. A shared expression of love. Awakened humanity's shared home upon the loving lands of Pachamama.

Collectively, humanity purged the Earth of all evil and rebirthed it anew. But individually, as souls, they first had to purge themselves of their own evil and arrive at the dimension of their own Heaven.

Each human being had his or her own tale, their own hero's journey of becoming that needed to be conquered.

It was not one human soul that saved the Earth dreamscape from evil, but every human soul who followed their uniquely aligned path. When humanity was ready, each unique mission unified into the collective singular mission, and the instantaneous rebirth was done.

Chapter Twenty-Four

And so, the tale of the dreamscape appears to have drawn to a close, but in reality it remains wide open. You, my dear friend, and I exist within the dreamscape.

A few months ago I met with Drew, my Vedic astrologer who had warned me of the lien against the boutique hotel in Bali that Scott and I were so close to buying. In this recent reading, Drew asked me if I was writing a book. At the time, I was not. My last burst of writing was over three years ago. No new inspiration to write was moving through me. Drew told me I was entering a window of time that would be very supportive for writing. And just like that, he planted a seed in my consciousness—just like the seed Jane planted in Jerry's consciousness.

Shortly after my reading with Drew, sentences began formulating in my head. Stories from my life began circulating through my vision in pictorial detail. And for the first time in three years, I opened my computer to write. Day by day, I was called back to my favourite writing spot in the dining room overlooking the valley through an oversized window. Each day of writing has been a mystery. Each character, each twist in the plot—it has just spontaneously arisen and flowed from my infinite consciousness into the keyboard.

Perhaps I would have written all this regardless of my session with Drew, or perhaps not. But time and time again in my life, wise friends, healers and psychics have planted visionary seeds in my consciousness that have eventually grown into trees of bountiful harvest.

Today as I sit and write, my heart is open, and I can hear the whispers of my innate connection to Spirit speaking through me. Is it the Eternal Ocean of Light or the Great Mother? It is both—unified as one—the loving spark of creation that is eternal oneness. That which I call the Divine.

The Divine is flooding me with waves of loving energy as a type. And now, I will write as a scribe and channel for the Divine. This message is for you, dear friend.

. . .

Beloved child,

We have shared a story with you, since we know how your minds love to dream and play. You are indeed living within a dreamscape at a pivotal moment in time. A choice point approaches, and the outcome for humanity lies within your capable hands.

The choice point does not exist within a certain day, month or year of your calendar. The choice point exists within the inner realm of your heart. Do you choose love? Or do you choose fear?

Must you rise to be a warrior and take up arms? No, battle is not required for love to be victorious. Love is required for love to be victorious. Have you not proven to yourself, time and time again, that you are indeed, love?

Now read this slowly, dear child. This message is important. You have received a roadmap to humanity's salvation through this tale. The details of your inevitable victory are laid out within the story.

All you need to do is look within.

Look within to heal the traumas of old hurts. Like Dario, follow guidance that shows you your sanctuary for letting go. And then, let it all go. The great purge is here for all of humanity—and it is here for you. The hurt of your past cannot be carried forward. The hurts of humanity's past must not be carried forward. Release it all. Nothing in your past is real, so free it from the truth of your eternal now. Be here now—infinite and whole—and ask of your heart: How can I assist the world around me from my anchored loving wholeness?

Like Beth, choose life on Earth fully. Give yourself to your incarnation. It is the most sacred gift you will ever receive. Relish the wonders of your human experience. Dance, sing and play often and don't forget to fall back in love with the trees, butterflies, flowers and oceans. Make love, cartwheel on the grass and eat the foods that make your taste buds come alive with pleasure. Earth is a paradise playground—so play. And as you give yourself to life fully, without resistance, you will merge so absolutely with each sacred moment that portals around you and within you will open, and help from unseen realms will flood to you and through you, showing you the way.

Seed visions in your consciousness of a spectacular future, beyond your wildest dreams, as Jane did for Jerry. Connect with your soul, and ask yourself, what does my soul long to experience in this incarnation? Seed yourself with a vision that excites you as a creative being. And then, like Jane, trust the timing of the stars. Your mission coexists with your most exquisite vision for your future—and your mission was never intended to be fulfilled in one day, but in the entire journey that is your incarnation. Seed the vision. Trust the timing. Give yourself to the mystery of the journey.

And then, train yourself to become diligently unwavering in your trust in the inevitable unfolding of your most cherished dream for the future. When Jane seeded Jerry with a vision for mass healings, Jerry didn't know the plan, but he gave his life in radical trust of the outcome. Unwavering trust accelerates your vision into manifest form. Master your mind into unwavering trust. Heal your body into unwavering trust. Doubt is fear. Trust is love. You are here on this Earth for a reason, and the reason is intertwined with the creative essence that makes you feel most alive. Do not judge your own free-flowing expression. That which makes you feel most alive is enough; in fact, it is why you are here. Your path of creative innocence is calling you home.

Your impact is equal to the expression of your free-flowing aliveness.

As your vision for your most exquisite future crystallises in your consciousness, you will be guided to fulfil that vision. You will be guided to confront your inner demons so that you can rise up as the impactful expression of love you were born to be. As you slay your inner demons, you will recognise the demonic expressions of fear all around you. And like Grace, the tiny woman with the courage of a lion, you will become a master alchemist who assists in the collective purge of the Earth realm from demonic infiltration. Humanity has a shared mission—a collective exorcism. And your training for this shared mission begins with the courageous work you do within. As you expose your hidden fears and chart the darkest corners of your own inner mechanisms, remember there is no power in fear, only in love. So train yourself to hold compassion for the aspects of yourself you had previously deemed unlovable. And in doing so, you prepare yourself to see the truth at the root of collective evil—fear, trauma and pain. Humanity's liberation is instantaneous when collectively you are anchored in love.

Your voice is a sacred tool to assist you to anchor in love and free yourself from fear. Just as Anna's voice could harmonise the frequency of the entire dreamscape, your voice can harmonise your own energy body. The power of your voice in its ability to liberate exists within your primal unfiltered sound. A refined and perfected singing voice does not liberate—authentic expression liberates. Find the teachers who can help you unblock your throat. When your throat is open, energy can move. Clearing your throat from lifetimes of suppression will require you to find from within the depths of yourself the primal sounds of your liberation. A liberated voice is a liberated body—and a liberated body is connected to truth at all levels.

These steps are the steps you must take individually to anchor yourself in love, so that collectively the Earth and humanity can rebirth itself into a new paradigm of shared Heaven.

You have been introduced to six aspects of the Sacred Seven:

Dario is you following the path of relentless self-healing that leads to selfless service to others.

Beth is you merging with the magic of incarnation in its multidimensional wholeness.

Jane is you seeding yourself with vision for the future and trusting the divine timing of the journey of life.

Jerry is you relentlessly following your own unique creative path with unwavering trust in the inevitable manifestation of your most cherished vision.

Grace is you and the courage of love that you will find as you continue to face all fears.

Anna is you and the power of your authentic expression to harmonise distortion and purify your body and the world around you.

These six aspects are all aspects of you. Aspects that you have initiated within yourself and will continue to strengthen.

The seventh and final aspect of the Sacred Seven is the aspect that has been revealed to you through Rhiannon, the scribe of this story—the storyteller, the dream weaver. You too are a sacred storyteller and dream weaver. It is of paramount importance that you initiate the storyteller within now. It is time to dream up a tale of a new Earth—a paradise for all. Your imagination is the only limitation of what is possible. A collective new beginning is yours for the taking—and it begins with your imagined and shared story of a spectacular future for all.

The world you perceive is a dream anyway, so dream tales of a new Earth into being—harmonious, liberated and free. Share these tales with your children; speak these dreamed stories into the imaginations of all who will listen. It is through storytelling that humanity collectively dreams wonder into manifest reality.

When did you stop dreaming stories of a wildly magnificent future for a new Earth? It's time to dream again. A shared Heaven on Earth begins with a shared story.

So, sit around the fire, as your ancestors did—dream and envision a paradise of Heaven on Earth through shared stories told to the glow of flickering ancient fire. Together, humanity is dreaming a new Earth into form, and the details of its beauty exist in the wonder of limitless imagination.

Humanity is arriving at a choice point—fear or love. Together, you will dream into form a world built upon the fabric of love. Your imagination is boundless, and within it exists the creative power of the Divine. Your stories told around the fire from here on will be a co-creation of your shared Heaven on Earth. It's coming. In fact, it is already here—and it is glorious.

www.ingramcontent.com/pod-product-compliance
Lightning Source LLC
LaVergne TN
LVHW091542060526
838200LV00036B/678